THE MAIDEN AND THE MOUNTIE

THE TWENTY-NINERS OF THE GEORGIA GOLD RUSH
BOOK TWO

DENISE FARNSWORTH   WRITING AS   DENISE WEIMER

WILD HEART BOOKS

Cover design by Evelyne Labelle at Carpe Librum Book Design. www.carpelibrumbookdesign.com

Print ISBN:978-1-963212-50-1

CHAPTER 1

OCTOBER 16, 1837

"Sergeant Edwards, you're needed for a mission of the greatest urgency."

The youthful yet earnest voice outside his tent had Gage pulling up his suspenders and pushing aside the canvas flap without so much as his waistcoat to break the early-morning chill. A mission the day after Buffington's Company of Georgia Mounted Militia arrived in Cherokee County? Before morning muster? It must be important. And that was why he was here— a chance to prove himself and to help his step-grandmother's Cherokee people.

He found the new acting assistant quartermaster planted outside his tent. The man was just as stiff and about as lean as the post. "What is it, Private Wood?" Gage slipped his arms into his woolen vest.

The youth snapped off a salute, which Gage returned. "The corn we hauled from New Echota has to be taken to the mill." He swiveled to wave toward the parade ground. "The sacks are still in the wagon. The ostler is hitchin' the team as we speak."

Gage slid the last pewter button of his waistcoat through its hole. "*This* is the urgent mission?"

John Wood shrugged. "Men have to eat, sir. That corn's the army's gold."

"Then why aren't you taking it, Assistant Quartermaster Wood?" The question sneaked out of him like a minnow through a fish trap.

"I'm helping set up the meal tent. Besides, Captain Buffington wanted an experienced military man to take the shipment...in case there's trouble. He has a particular interest because he supplied the corn himself."

Gage frowned. "Is trouble expected?" If so, he'd request Donald McCleary ride shotgun. He trusted the no-nonsense Scotsman to be cool under fire above any other private in the company.

"Nothing beyond what might be expected for soldiers of an occupyin' army." Wood's chortle drew Gage's brows even closer together.

"We're not here to occupy, Private. We're here to protect."

"Right, sir. Whatever you say, sir." Wood shifted impatiently. "In any case, the captain specifically asked for you."

He did? Gage weighed that information, sliding his forefinger over the slight bristle that covered his chin. He'd been with the Gainesville Dragoons in the spring campaign against the Seminoles last year, but did Captain Buffington know his record? Was that why Gage was chosen for an assignment the drummer boy could carry out?

When they'd been stationed at the Cherokee capital where they'd received their training, he'd not been chosen to accompany Lieutenant Clayton to pursue the murderer of a native man in Walker County. Or to investigate the depredations against Cherokees in Paulding County. The rising fear in his gut that he'd been enlisted as a sergeant as a nod to his father's military renown battled with the humility his faith and his godly mother had instilled in him. Who was he to think he deserved anything? He'd have to earn a chance to prove himself. And he could start by driving the corn to the mill.

He dropped his hand and gave a brief nod. "My apologies, Private. It will be my honor to carry out Captain Buffington's request. Just where is this mill located?"

Private Wood gestured to the Alabama Road—deserted and barely visible in dawn's gray haze—where it ran near their camp, which would soon enough be Fort Buffington. "'Bout a quarter mile west toward Canton, you'll find a lane running south to Mill Creek. Walker Mill sits on Walker Creek, a tributary. Should be signs. Now, if I can beg your leave..."

"Of course. Thank you, Private Wood." After the assistant quartermaster returned his salute and skedaddled back toward the cooking tent, Gage let out a sigh and re-entered his temporary lodgings to finish dressing.

Ezekiel Buffington was right to safeguard the corn. His company could hardly be expected to build a palisade, barracks, stables, and blockhouses on empty stomachs. Fort Buffington was to be the supply depot for the westernmost encampments in a chain of over a dozen forts established under General Wool. The mounted troops manning the forts operated under his orders to protect the lives and property of the Cherokee people until the deadline for their removal next spring.

Many good citizens protested the plans of the government —pushed by the greed of settlers seeking gold since its discovery in these parts eight or so years prior—to move the peaceful Cherokees west to Oklahoma Territory. To take land that had sustained them for decades. The notion was especially egregious to men like Gage's father, who credited the victory at Horseshoe Bend against the British-allied Creek Indians to the Cherokee Regiment he'd been honored to fight alongside during the War of 1812. Which was one reason Gage's opportunity to serve here was so vital. After what had happened in Florida, Gage owed his father a debt that reached beyond the grave.

Though a trip to the mill would likely offer little of interest besides viewing the machinery, Gage would dedicate himself wholeheartedly to whatever he found there.

By the time he'd shaved and donned his boots and overcoat, the musician had sounded reveille. The low hum of male voices permeated the camp as men prepared for their first roll call on land owned by local farmer Moses Perkins. The clank of metal indicated that their farrier and blacksmith was somehow already at work despite the lack of an established forge. Gage slung his cartridge box over his shoulder and reached for his musket before exiting his tent. He found the wagon loaded and waiting as Private Wood had described.

The smoke from campfires mingled with the lingering morning mist as he pulled the team onto the Alabama Road and headed west minutes later. Gage unwrapped his biscuit and jerky to consume his morning meal as he jounced along. He'd little distance to go before the turnoff onto what was likely to be a narrow lane requiring both hands on the reins. This land was not so different from his home. Gainesville's rolling hills commanded distant mountain views, but this area, with its deep woodlands, gold-rich rivers, and ridges that stunned one with unexpected vistas, would surely make the Cherokee loath to leave.

Clouds of tiny white and lavender asters lined the road while stalks of goldenrod studded the fields. When he made the turn to Walker Mill, the forest in its autumnal glory enclosed him. Russet dogwoods and golden poplars and maples competed for his attention like ladies parading on a boardwalk. The pokewood stalks and berries had purpled, and the mimosas dangled rustling leather pods over the lane. Not to be outdone, the sourwood and blackberry leaves glowed like a red woolen petticoat flung amongst the underbrush.

As he neared Walker Creek, a few homesteads broke the heavy forest canopy—dew on the pumpkins, stalk leavings in cornfields, and neat log cabins and outbuildings set in dirt clearings. Bottle gourds attracted nesting martins as they stood like sentries over gardens with pale-style or woven cane fencing. Some homes had potato houses on high ground and springhouses near the creek.

Gage shook his head. Despite their European design, most of these spreads probably belonged to Cherokees. Just another travesty of this scheduled removal was the fact that the tribe had adopted many ways of their white neighbors, down to their own newspaper and legal system. Missionaries had long been at work among the people, starting schools and churches.

Sudden unease clenched in his gut. He hadn't considered that the mill might be owned by Cherokees. How would they feel about grinding corn for the army?

Troops had been stationed in the area for years—mostly east of here. If he remembered correctly, they'd been near the inn owned by Jacob Scudder, a white man considered a blood brother to the Cherokees. But while some of the native population appreciated the protection from gold-hungry winners of the lottery designed to divvy up their land, others saw their presence much as Private Wood had described...as that of an occupying force. A reminder that, should the efforts of Cherokee leaders fail to convince Washington to help, the same soldiers would be called on to forcibly remove those who had not already chosen to depart for the West. Gage had every intention of mustering out before that happened.

The music of the creek trilled above the creak and jingle of the wagon as the lane widened into a dirt yard that supported the mill complex, which included a log cabin and outbuildings much like those he'd just passed. Gage drew the team to a halt to admire the picturesque view. Walker Creek had been partially dammed above a natural shoal. A box raceway using a gate system channeled the flow to the top of a massive wooden overshot wheel attached to the back of the two-story frame mill building, and currently sat silent.

Sight of another wagon in front of the mill and two men standing before the half-open Dutch door spoiled Gage's hopes that he might be the first customer. He parked alongside the other vehicle and set his brake. Only then did the raised voices reach his ears.

"You can't deny me service! I got the same rights as any customer." Shadowed by a thin younger man, a stocky middle-aged man whose battered black hat covered most of what his grizzled brown beard failed to conceal shook his fist at two boys who stood behind the lower portion of the door.

"I can deny you service if you bring less than the required portion." Emotion made the reply of the youth in an equally floppy hat more than a bit unsteady as he tipped his head toward the small bag the man held. And judging by the tenor, the owner of the voice wasn't much older than the boy who hung back just behind him, his head just reaching the older one's shoulder.

If the boys found the courage to stand up to two full-grown men, there must be a good reason. Gage climbed down and reached behind the seat for his musket.

The irate customer lowered his arms to his sides. "Where's your father?"

That's what Gage wanted to know.

"At a meeting. If my terms don't please you, you can try the mills at Sixes or Scudder's." The youth squared his shoulders. White, then, judging by the diction and the lack of nasal sound that Cherokees often had when speaking English—though the slighter boy who watched the exchange with wide eyes had the tawny look of a half blood. Hired help, perhaps?

"Yeah. Maybe we should go, Uncle Isaiah." The younger man with shoulder-length blond hair and a rangy height spoke for the first time. He ventured a nudge to his companion's arm.

The one called Isaiah threw him off with an explosive curse. "I ain't goin' miles outta my way when we got a mill right here." He stepped closer to the building. "Or maybe it only serves *certain kinds* of customers."

"Is there a problem here?" Gage moved into the man's line of sight so he could no longer be ignored.

Finally, Isaiah shot him a look. "Sure is. Can't get no service at my own local mill."

"This is the third time he's come with below the portion we require to run the machinery." Disgust roughened the voice of the miller's son, whose face flashed in Gage's direction, although he still stood in the shadows as though ready to turn away at any moment. "My father let him get away with it the first two times because he didn't want trouble. But there won't be a third."

The blond turned to his relative. "Is that true, Uncle?"

The older man ignored his nephew as he spluttered his indignation. "Oh, there won't, will there? We'll see what you have to say when—"

"Isn't the machinery running at all hours in harvest season?" Gage moved closer to the miller's boy.

The wearer of the black hat gave a brief nod. "But he bets on the fact that my father won't charge a toll if he's under the amount. Everybody knows Isaiah Thompson's a cheat."

"Why, you..." Thompson lunged forward, reaching over the top of the Dutch door and grabbing the boy by his muslin shirt before Gage could react. Thompson shook the youth, bumping him against the doorframe. The boy's hat fell off, revealing two long, dark braids and the prettiest features Gage had ever laid eyes on.

The miller's son was...a woman?

CHAPTER 2

The tall stranger who'd pulled up in the mill yard moments after Anna Walker's unwelcome customers had arrived jerked Isaiah Thompson back from the door. She exhaled a quick puff of breath as his grip broke free. What would she have done if the newcomer hadn't arrived? She'd have sent Ned for her musket propped against the toll booth, that's what.

Her nephew picked up her fallen hat. "You all right, *Etlogi*?"

"Yes, fine." Her attention focused on the drama unfolding outside her door, where only Micah Thompson's quick reflexes prevented his uncle from swinging his fist at the interfering stranger.

The newcomer now gripped his musket in both hands before him. At least he hadn't pointed it at Isaiah, though Anna could hardly blame him if he did. He lowered it slowly, brows drawn low under an unusual white felt hat, the type she'd noticed several newcomers wearing of late. "Best you men be moving on."

"Nobody asked for your opinion. Or your meddlin'." Micah

spat his reply and shot Anna a hot glance, no doubt riled the stranger had come to her aid before he could. "Sorry, Anna. I didn't know he'd been here before. Let's go, Uncle. We'll come back when we have a full load."

"Come back, my rheumatic hound!" Isaiah flung out a hand. "Naw. I'll be tellin' all the decent folk in these parts to go elsewhere to have their meal ground. And you..." He turned his steely gaze on the stranger. "Don't you get in my way again."

The man straightened to what must be over six feet of lithe and muscular height, drawing his musket to his side. "I could say the same...Mr. Thompson. Or you'll have the mounted militia to reckon with."

Anna's heart sank like a stone to the bottom of the millpond. Heat licked up from her belly. Had she really entertained, even for a moment, the notion of some hero riding in to protect her? How foolish. Given the fact that he was a soldier, utterly contemptible. But how could she have known, when even the militia officers often dressed more like frontier hunters?

Without stopping to think what she was doing or how her father would react, she swung the top of the Dutch door shut, slid the bolt board into place, and marched over to the ledger. She flipped the heavy book open. Ned trailed behind her, frowning.

A moment later, the latch rattled without effect. Anna's stomach twinged with guilt. A knock came on the heavy wooden door.

Ned started for the entrance, but she jerked him back by his floppy collar.

He rounded on her with wide eyes, dark as obsidian. "What you doing, Aunt Anna?" She'd startled him into using her English title. She preferred Etlogi. "His wagon was full of corn. We make the soldier mad."

Anna chewed her lip. *Agidoda* would have her hide if he learned she'd turned away such a well-paying customer...and the army, at that.

The knock came again. She blindly shuffled pages. The only way her father knew which customers came in his absence was if she recorded something. But what if the soldier reported their unwillingness to serve him?

"I know you're in there."

The rich, deep tone was all the more effective for its patience and control. Her stomach flipped over. He thought to command her without even raising his voice. The army was worse than the miners. The only thing worse than the army was the Pony Club, which terrorized Cherokees who had the gumption to hold onto their land this long after the lottery.

Her enemy spoke again. "The Thompsons have gone, and I mean you no harm. I only want my corn ground. I'm on orders from my captain. Open up, please?"

A gentleman—likely an officer, if his cultured speech gave any indication. Forget grinding corn. Anna was too busy grinding her teeth. Finally, she nodded at Ned, who had waited poised halfway between her and the threshold. He scuttled over to open the door—the entire thing this time.

The soldier stood a moment framed by the golden morning light, a canvas sack balanced on his broad shoulder. He closed the bottom half of the door meant to keep out stray animals and swept off his hat—which she now realized was unusual because it was part of a makeshift uniform, along with the cartridge box over his shoulder. As he bowed his head, a lock of his thick, wavy brown hair fell over his forehead. He looked up. Those green eyes, like jade—*u-yo-i*. No good.

"Sergeant Gage Edmonds, miss." He contained the strand within the circumference of his headwear as he stepped forward, but not before his eyebrows disappeared under the rim. He'd gotten a gander at her trousers, then.

Anna refused to acknowledge his astonishment with so much as a brush of her hand against the men's wool pantaloons she wore beneath her shortened skirt—more of a tunic, really, as it lacked the volume of ladies' skirts. She gestured instead to the scale on the floor. "You may place your corn there."

He spoke as he did so. "Ten more bags like this." When she raised an eyebrow, he added, "It's already been shelled, if that helps."

He was probably accustomed to making the young ladies knock-kneed. She firmed her legs in protest. "I will take that into account." She wrote the date, his name, and the weight of the first bag in the ledger. "Will a one-tenth toll be acceptable?" This she asked without meeting his gaze again.

And why was she using her best English? Like a proper lady. His courtly manner seemed to call it forth, as if she had to prove to him that she could be his equal. She ought to break into a stream of Cherokee and see how he reacted then. But she rather liked the challenge of showing him how genteel she could be, despite the unconventional garb and setting.

He dipped his head. "I believe that's standard."

"It is." Anna opened the bag and used her wooden scoop to transfer the allotted portion to the toll box that sat beneath her ledger desk. "Regular cornmeal, sir?"

"Yes, please."

Good. The millstones were already set to grind to that consistency. She bent to reach for the remaining corn.

Before she could lift it, Sergeant Edmonds swooped in and did so. "Where do you want it?"

She flushed. "I'm perfectly capable of lifting a ten-pound bag." She couldn't let him think she lacked the ability to run the mill in her father's absence.

"I'm sure you are, but one man has already shown himself to be a cur this morning. I'd like your experience with the next one to be more pleasant, especially as I represent my superiors." Accompanied by those unexpected words, the flash of his white teeth and his laugh lines rattled her so much, she turned away.

She caught her nephew's eye. "Ned, you may do the honors this morning."

The eleven-year-old seized the opportunity to accomplish his favorite task and hopped onto the millstone platform to turn the metal wheel that would open the sluice gate and start the mill's operation. A moment later, water roared down the raceway, followed by the *thump-thump-thump* as the great wheel started to turn. Her heart always seemed to align with the sound, as though it now beat with the community's lifeblood. The building vibrated as the great metal gears beneath them groaned and resumed their faithful operation.

A flush of a different nature now warmed her...contentment. This was her purpose. She'd far rather be here every day than hearthside. How fortunate she was to have a father who understood that.

The rattle of kernels drew her attention back to the gentlemanly sergeant. He'd poured the contents of his bag into the raised bin beside her. At her startled look, he widened his eyes slightly. "That was right, wasn't it? The receiving hopper?"

"Yes."

He correctly read her incredulity. "I have been to a mill before, Miss Thompson. Shall I fetch the other bags?"

She gave a nod and began to move the first metal screen back and forth in its wooden frame, channeling the corn to the next filter to remove unwanted debris. By the time he'd returned with the next two bags, she had pulled the lever to release the grain into the basement. From there, with a noisy hum and clatter, it traveled in its little wooden scoops up the heavy woven belt to the attic, where a blower removed any remaining chaff before dropping it onto one of two millstones on the platform behind her. Ned took up his post overseeing the grinding and positioning a canvas sack beneath the shoot to the receiving bin.

To her consternation, Sergeant Edmonds insisted on lifting every bag to and from the scale and receiving hopper. Even with her willowy height, he loomed over her, taller than most Cherokee men. With each transaction, she moved the peg at the side of her desk to tally the total and bit her tongue to keep from telling him his gallantry was slowing her down. Not to mention, his presence so close set her on edge—that smell of man and spice and horse. Those green eyes seeking her approval before he completed each step. At last, she could stand it no longer. "I believe you can start loading your meal, sir." The *sir* provided a nice shield.

He assessed her for a moment, then wandered back toward the millstone platform where Ned was bagging grain. Instead of taking the meal to his wagon, he clasped his hands behind him and leaned back to study the shoot spewing grain from the ceiling. "An impressive operation you have here. I'd love to see the inner workings."

In the process of sifting the last batch of kernels, Anna stiffened. He wanted a tour? Not on her watch. She continued sifting, pretending not to hear over the rattle, hum, and thump of machinery.

"How long have you been in operation?"

"What?" She paused with a frown, then raised her voice. "I'm sorry—I can't hear you over the noise." With a dismissive shake of her head, she went back to what she was doing.

"I said, 'How long have you been in operation?'" Louder this time.

"My father built the mill when I was five...in 1820."

His brows shot up, alerting her that she'd unwittingly revealed her age...something a proper lady would never do. "Indeed? It would seem we share the same year of birth."

So he was also twenty-two? Young for a man. Far past the

age to marry for a woman. And she'd daresay, their only thing in common.

He drifted closer again. "I assume you help your father here often?" He gave a nod to her attire.

She resisted the urge to bristle. "It would be foolish to scamper about a mill in ruffles and petticoats."

Once again, his grin blinded her. "Imminently impractical."

Anna had grown accustomed to derision, especially from newcomers, as the locals had adjusted to the clothing she wore in the mill. But approval? Disarming. Yet being disarmed was the last thing she needed from this soldier.

She pulled her shoulders back. "My father is an important man in the community. He has meetings to attend and business to conduct." Especially now, as their people fought harassment from white settlers and eviction from their land. But she wouldn't detail that to this man. To her immense relief, wheels creaking in the yard signaled a wagon pulling up before the mill. She tipped her head to the Dutch door. "It seems Ned has finished bagging your order just in time."

He sidled closer. "I wanted to tell you—"

"Thank you for your business, Sergeant Edwards." Anna headed for the threshold.

"Edmonds." He mumbled the correction, but when she opened the door for a local farmer, the sergeant finally turned to collect his order.

Already weighing her neighbor's grain, she didn't spare the soldier a glance as he passed her on his way to the door. She had enough to contend with, putting off the attentions of Micah Thompson, the last suitor she'd ever welcome. Not to mention trying to keep their home running and property safe. Hopefully, the cornmeal they'd provided today would keep the army satisfied for many weeks. She had no need to nurture any sort of relationship with Sergeant Edmonds. Regardless of what she had said, his name had been burned on her mind the moment she wrote it in the ledger, like a brand that wouldn't go away.

He might not yet know that Walker could be a Cherokee name, but she'd do well to remember he was here to take the mill away from her. Whatever game the charming mountie was playing would not end well for her. It never did.

CHAPTER 3

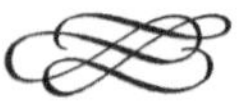

On Gage's first Sunday morning in Cherokee Territory, the arrival of two fair-skinned ladies in bright calico dresses and flower-trimmed bonnets drew his attention to the rear of the small rustic schoolhouse at the former Tinsawattee Baptist Mission. And not just because they might be the only other people in the room besides him not of Cherokee descent. He'd expected to stand out when he'd elected to attend the service here given by a native lay speaker rather than First Baptist Church in Canton. The mission had been established just west of town by Reverend Duncan O'Bryant before he followed an early party of Cherokee refugees to Oklahoma. Now the complex nestled among the hardwoods in a curve of the Alabama Road was only used for community gatherings and when itinerant preachers came through. Neither did the ladies hold his eye because they were exceptionally striking in appearance. Rather, because the younger one in deep green was Anna Walker.

He'd been unable to expunge her from his thoughts all week. Indeed, he'd asked his lieutenant if he might not need to ride by the mill to make certain no further trouble brewed there. Unfortunately, the officer had found the complaints of a disgruntled farmer less than a military threat.

Gage had to admit, his own sense of urgency stemmed as much from a burning desire to figure out why she had brushed him off when he'd come to her aid and then done everything in his power to be gentlemanly and show polite interest. It stung his manly pride a bit. Had he said something unwittingly offensive? Or was she normally so brusque? Her unconventional attire had taken him aback at first, but then he'd been struck by the notion of a female with the bent to run a mill—which she'd proceeded to do quite efficiently.

And now here she was, slipping onto a back bench and looking as fine a lady as ever he saw. Was her companion her mother? What were they doing here—a significant ride from their mill, and in a congregation predominantly Cherokee? A nicely dressed middle-aged man with lightly bronzed skin trailed in behind them, then sat on the men's side.

When Gage's gaze swung back to Miss Walker, her eyes met his for a second and widened. He gave a slight but intentional nod. She quickly looked away.

A broad-shouldered black man rose from the end of Gage's bench, welcomed them in English and Cherokee, and encouraged them to consult the paper given out upon their arrival to sing the first hymn. Clothing rustled and benches squeaked as everyone stood. The song leader sounded the first note to signal the key. The hymn in Cherokee, rendered a cappella in four-note style, reverberated off the chinked log walls. Despite the fact that Gage could make little sense of the native tongue written on the page he clutched, the song was oddly stirring. *Unisi* had only taught him to speak the language, not to read it. Thankfully, the tune of "O God Our Help in Ages Past" provided enough direction for him to get in a word here and there.

Even more fortuitous, once they sat down, Brother Sweetwater delivered the message, alternating between Cherokee and English. Gage found himself hastening to decipher every word before the lay minister could offer the translation. The deep grunting sound that was part of Cherokee oratory and preceded a pause usually gave enough time for Gage to catch onto the meaning. The creation story from Genesis was easy enough to follow. Not so much, the veiled references to those in the community who spread rumors that the Cherokees joining the Christian faith went against the government. That made no sense at all.

Gage even forgot Miss Walker...until the final hymn. Was he wrong, or did he feel her eyes upon him as he rose? Likely, his wishful thinking. At the mill, the young lady had made her disdain for him more than clear.

Nevertheless, he could not stop himself from stepping quickly into the aisle in an attempt to catch her before she exited. By a stroke of fortune, several other ladies had detained her and her companion where they sat. So as not to be obvious, Gage slipped down the aisle past them without a glance and went to shake Brother Sweetwater's hand. The broad-chested, middle-aged man wore the go-to-meeting garb of a white settler, complete with a dark frock coat and white stock. The man's face was carefully blank as he released Gage's hand. But Unisi's instruction had proven sound enough that Gage found the courage to thank him in Cherokee for the sermon.

Sweetwater's thick brows rose as Gage spoke. "You have quite the command of our tongue." He glanced pointedly at the white felt hat under Gage's arm. "For a soldier."

Gage smiled. "Aginisi taught me." At the other man's surprised blink, he added, "Second wife to my grandfather. Not blood."

"Ah." Sweetwater nodded. "A man in your position could do great service for our people."

"That is my hope." Though he had yet to determine fully *how*.

As if reading his mind, the preacher continued, still talking in Cherokee, though more slowly than he likely would have had he been communicating with another native speaker. "You can start by telling everyone the government favors our Christian religion. Then invite them to the meetings here. In December, Brother Bushyhead will return."

"Brother Bushyhead?" Gage kept his gaze trained on his companion although a flash of green calico on the steps behind him tempted his eye.

"Our Cherokee brother from North Carolina who travels the Baptist circuit with Reverend Evan Jones. He is a far more gifted speaker than I. Spread the word. Invite your soldier friends." Brother Sweetwater shook Gage's hand, his grip firm. "Reverend Jones gives his sermon in English."

"Thank you. I will." Some of the militiamen could use a dose of the Gospel. There'd been incidents of theft, drinking, and visiting women of ill repute during their time stationed at New Echota. It would only be a matter of time before men given to such vices sought them out in this community.

"Good. Please excuse me." Brother Sweetwater turned to greet Anna Walker and the woman with her. "Thank you for coming, Miss Walker. Mrs. Campbell." He'd switched to English. And the use of different names told Gage the women were not related, after all. "Did you find the service helpful?"

"Oh, very." Moving with the grace of an upper-class lady and the authority of middle years, Mrs. Campbell gripped the lay speaker's hand. "Especially so in repudiating the ridiculous claims of that conjurer at Long Swamp and his ilk. Your point that God is the great judge to whom we are ultimately answerable was especially well received."

"A conjurer?" The question escaped Gage before he could consider it an interruption to the new conversation. Thankfully, he stood near enough that no one gawped at him when they turned their notice upon him.

Brother Sweetwater shrugged. "A poor attempt to deter the spread of the Gospel."

"Not so poor. Father and I have noticed a drop in attendance at preaching services since summer." Miss Walker shifted to allow the mixed-blood man Gage had noticed earlier to join her. She slipped her hand into the crook of the gentleman's arm as he nodded to Brother Sweetwater. "It's why we were determined to come this morning."

Father? Gage blinked as the gears in his head turned as slowly as the mill's must on a frosty morning. Yes. Miss Walker's stare bore into him with an unmistakable directness, almost a challenge. He hadn't done anything offensive last week. His mere presence as a sergeant in the Georgia Mounted Militia had been what stuck in her craw.

And she...she was part Cherokee? Yes, she possessed dark hair and eyes and finely sculpted facial features, but her skin was lily white, and traces of a reddish hue glimmered in her silky locks. He never would've guessed it. And now, she seemed to be enjoying having taken him off guard. Her full lips pressed together with a hint of a smirk, then she said, "It's Sergeant Edwards whose company is a surprise." An unwelcome one, judging by the emphasis she placed on the mispronunciation of his name.

Gage didn't provide the satisfaction of correcting her. Instead, he merely dipped his head. "Miss Walker."

"You know each other?" Mrs. Campbell's dark-blond brows flirted with the brim of her bonnet.

Miss Walker pursed her lips, making a dimple in her cheek flash for the briefest of moments. "The sergeant brought the army's corn to the mill this past week."

Mrs. Campbell blinked as though Miss Walker had called

Gage General Wool. "Well, someone simply must introduce me."

"Sergeant, this is Mrs. Peggy Campbell." Brother Sweetwater extended his hand toward the stately woman. "Mrs. Campbell runs an inn between Canton and your encampment."

"Pleased to make your acquaintance, ma'am." Gage offered a respectful bow.

As soon as he straightened, Anna's father spoke. "Her husband is of the Red Bank Village just west of here, as I am. In fact, he is a distant relative."

But her last name was Campbell? The quick glance Gage shot her must have betrayed his curiosity.

A smile flitted about her lips. "For the sake of business, I kept the last name of my first husband."

"Ah." He dipped his head. That made sense.

Anna's father stepped forward, extending his hand. When Gage took it, the man clasped his palm in a firm grip that lingered while he spoke. "Joshua Walker. My daughter told me of your visit to our mill. I regret I was away, but I wish to thank you for coming to her aid."

Only when Mr. Walker finally loosened his grip did Gage drop his hand and step back. "She told you about that?" He couldn't resist a peek at Miss Walker, who lifted her chin before she replied.

"As I mentioned, it wasn't the first time the Thompsons caused trouble."

Gage addressed her father again as Brother Sweetwater excused himself to greet other congregants. "I'm glad to make your acquaintance, sir. I want to assure you, the militia is here to protect you during this time of transition."

"Until the removal deadline, you mean." There was no mistaking the rancor in Mrs. Campbell's tone or stiff posture.

Gage flushed. Apparently, her property had not belonged to

her previous husband, and through his will, to her. With her current spouse being Cherokee or part Cherokee, no doubt, the land and its significant "improvements" had already been assigned to a winner of the 1833 land lottery who was waiting impatiently to claim their bounty.

Before he could reply, Miss Walker threaded her hands through Mrs. Campbell's elbow just beneath her puffed sleeve and spoke in a soft voice. "Shush. Didn't you hear that Chief Ross is making good progress fighting the removal bill in Washington? At the least, he'll buy us another two years."

Gage couldn't share her optimism. His father had forecasted the removal ever since President Andrew Jackson betrayed his former Cherokee allies by siding with the land-hungry, gold-mining settlers. Though Jackson's term had ended that spring, his successor, Martin Van Buren, supported Jacksonian policies. The army wouldn't be here building removal forts otherwise. The government had every intention of enforcing the Treaty of New Echota, signed in December of 1835 by only a small portion of prominent but non-official Cherokee leaders allied with Major John Ridge. The agreement exchanged their native lands for seven million acres in Northeast Oklahoma and five million dollars, to be carried out within two years.

But rather than argue with her, Gage offered a faint smile. "It is my fondest wish your leaders will be successful in their appeal, Miss Walker."

"And then what will you do, Sergeant Edwards? All that work for nothing."

Gage remained relaxed despite her sarcasm, lightly spoken as it was. "Why, I will return to my home in Gainesville content that I've done my duty to protect my Cherokee friends."

"You consider us friends?" Her lovely dark brows arched up like the wings of a small bird.

"I do, indeed." He tipped his head in deference. "My grandfather ran a trading post in Cherokee Territory after the Revolution. The nurse he brought home to my sickly grandmother and their infant son upon her death became a mother to my father. She raised him. His regard for your people was only furthered by their bravery when he served alongside them in the Red Stick War. It is in his memory that I serve now."

"That is how you know Cherokee." Her breathy observation was nearly lost in her father's statement as he stepped forward, his countenance enlivening.

"Your father fought in Creek Territory?"

"Yes, sir."

If possible, the man stood even straighter. "As did I."

Gage flashed a smile. "I would love to hear your account of it sometime and compare it to my father's. For now, do send word to me at the encampment if the Thompsons cause you further grief."

"Why not now?" The question Mr. Walker posed stopped Gage before he could don his hat and walk away.

"I'm sorry?"

"Why not come now?" He turned to his daughter, seeming not to notice the way her features were frozen in an expression somewhere between shock and horror. "You can heat that delicious stew you made last night, *Uwetsiageyv*." He placed a tender emphasis on the Cherokee word for *daughter*.

Miss Walker blinked innocently at him. "Oh...but Father, I'm sure there's not enough."

Mrs. Campbell covered a hint of laughter with a small cough.

"Nonsense. There was plenty." Mr. Walker drew his daughter's arm through his own again and patted it. "Besides, we wish to thank the sergeant for his assistance at the mill, do we not? It would be wise, in these times, to have soldiers for friends."

"I...we..." Miss Walker's panicked gaze lassoed Gage like that of a person about to fall off a cliff. But now it was Gage's turn to stand silent, pressing down a smile. He knew better than to refuse the offer of his Cherokee host—even to mollify the man's daughter. At length, the young lady sucked in a fortifying breath and said, "Of course, Father."

"In that case, it will be my pleasure." Gage gave a slight bow, unable to tamp down his enthusiasm at the prospect of spending the afternoon in her company.

She quirked her mouth to one side, making that enchanting dimple reappear—in more of a grimace than an expression of pleasure. "We shall see about that, Sergeant Edwards."

"So we shall, Miss *Walter*." He shot back a teasing smile, but why did the glint in her eye make him wonder what he was getting himself into?

CHAPTER 4

The admonishment Agidoda had given her while Sergeant Edmonds followed their wagon home from church on his glossy brown stallion wedged under her ribs like a sharp flint, prying every resentment up from the bottom of her heart. Treat the man with the utmost respect? Why should they respect the men trying to force them from their home? Pretend to be friends with them? The sergeant could say whatever he wished about protecting them from greedy settlers. He could play at being noble until the cows came home. The truth was, should Chief Ross fail in his political negotiations, Sergeant Edmonds would not hesitate to follow orders to evict them forcibly. Why did her father insist on hanging onto old allegiances?

The truth was, Gage Edmonds had about as much in common with them as his fancy thoroughbred did with their mule. And she'd prove it, both to him and her father.

She could only hope that word of this little visit didn't get back to Smoke Sanders at Hickory Log Village. Not when she'd finally succeeded in capturing his interest.

In the yard before their cabin, her father set the brake. "The sergeant and I will see to the horses, then come in for coffee while the stew heats."

"*V-v*. Yes, *Edoda*." He wanted her to lay a proper English spread for the guest. She had something else in mind, but she'd wait until they had an audience to play out her little scheme.

His brows lowered the slightest bit as he answered in a low tone. "Call me 'Father' today, and English, no Cherokee."

"But he speaks Cherokee." It would be interesting to see just how much. Would he know that the Cherokee name for Father changed from Edoda when she was talking to him to Agidoda when she was talking *about* him?

"Do not let your mother's training go to waste, *aqua danvdo*." Father's usual endearment for her, *my heart*, never ceased to work its will.

He rose and moved to assist her as she climbed down from the wagon, but both Anna's reply and her descent were interrupted when she turned almost directly into the broad chest of Sergeant Edmonds, who had somehow already dismounted and come to her aid. He stood so close, in fact, that she was forced to take his hand to steady herself as much from his nearness as from the step down from the wagon.

She refused to thank him for what she had not asked for, and she slid to one side and released his firm, gloved hand as quickly as possible. She smoothed her skirt and looked around rather than into those alert green eyes. "How do you find our little spread, Sergeant? Quite different from your home in Gainesville, I would imagine."

"I find it charming." His gaze took in their neat double-pen cabin with its dogtrot breezeway, located several hundred yards away from the mill. The scent of hickory from the smokehouse where they were currently drying corn and fish tinged the crisp air. Their hog grunted in his pen nearby, blissfully unaware that his days were numbered.

"Anna has been busy preparing us for winter when she is

not helping me at the mill." As he climbed down from the wagon, Father nodded toward the boards she used to sun-dry produce propped against the side of the house and the gourd containers on the front porch that held the beans she'd shelled from the garden. In fact, only a few pumpkins, winter squash, and cabbages remained in the once-burgeoning rows.

Sergeant Edmonds glanced between them. "Is it...just the two of you, then?"

Father came around the wagon. "Anna is the only child of my second wife, Mary. From my first Cherokee wife, I had a son and two daughters. All of them are married and live nearby. My son, Crow, works the land for us." Gone were the days when Cherokee women tended the fields while the men hunted and went to war. They had been taught the ways of white men. "So yes, in this house, it is just Anna and me."

"And your wife...Mary?"

Sorrow clouded Father's face. "She died at the end of Anna's first year at Salem College."

Sergeant Edmonds dipped his head. "I'm very sorry to hear that." The genuine sympathy he exuded as he encompassed her with his gaze left Anna unsettled.

Her father murmured his thanks, but she looked away.

"I still have my mother," Gage said, "but I lost my father not long ago, as well."

The tight statement drew her eyes to his. Not good. The haunted expression there intensified the fluttering in her midsection into an ache. She did not want to feel compassion for this man.

He took the opportunity her attention afforded to ask another question. "You attended college?" His expression lightened to one of admiration. Or more likely, surprise. That at least would be more welcome than admiration, which she needed no more than his sympathy.

While she would have only dipped her head, of course, her

father answered. "Anna began her studies in the Tinswattie School where we had our morning service. It was her mother's wish that she continue her education with the Moravian missionaries at Spring Place." Pride rang in his voice, causing heat to lick up her neck.

Sergeant Edmonds nodded. "I know it. The school at Chief Vann's plantation north of New Echota." The wealthy Cherokee leader and entrepreneur had invited the plain people from Salem, North Carolina, to start a school on his land just after the turn of the century.

"Yes. From there, she attended Salem College."

"I also was acquainted with a young lady who went there."

Was there no end to the sergeant's familiarity? Anna raised her brows, which he apparently took as an inquiry.

"Miss Sarah Ridge. Otherwise known as Sally. You know her?" He tilted his head as he gazed at Anna.

"I know *of* her." Who didn't? She was the daughter of Treaty Party leader Major John Ridge—not to mention, her reputation as the ideal pupil had preceded Anna at both Spring Place and Salem.

Sergeant Edmonds grinned as though she'd revealed Miss Ridge had been her best friend. "She married General Wool's aide-de-camp, Lieutenant George Paschal, from near here—Auraria, I believe—in February."

"Yes, and removed to Arkansas."

Her father overlooked her wry comment, instead resuming his commentary on her education. "Anna is among the best educated girls in Cherokee County, though she did not get to finish at Salem. She insisted on coming home when fever took her mother."

The corners of Sergeant Edmond's mouth lifted. "As any good daughter would." Yes...definitely admiration.

"I must put the coffee on." Anna backed away.

"Remember to set out some of that pound cake Mrs. Campbell taught you to make." Father turned to Sergeant Edmonds. "Did I tell you I met Anna's mother in Tennessee, before the war?"

"No. Her people were from there?"

"Yes. Her father, Captain Meade, served under General Jackson."

Sergeant Edmonds rubbed his chin. "That name sounds familiar…"

Anna left them to reminisce and tend the horses. She entered the cabin, tied on her apron, and stirred up the fire with her chest as hot as the coals. Sergeant Edmonds would learn her mother had come from a wealthy white family, giving him even more reason to suppose they had something in common. But that would only show how naïve he was. He had no idea what it was like to fit in nowhere—even at the schools her mother's family had paid for. And now her mother was dead, and the head of her household was a half-blood Cherokee, which meant her family stood to lose everything while the sergeant and men like him profited from their dispossession.

She lifted the pot of the stew she'd planned to serve for the midday meal, tipped the lid for a sniff, and wrinkled her nose. While there might be enough for three bowls, it surely smelled a bit rancid. Didn't it? She poured the contents into the slop pail and set the leftover bean bread on a skillet atop the coals next to the coffeepot.

Anna wiped her hands on her apron. Hm. Pound cake…

Not today. There was no way she aimed to aid Father's portrayal of her as a proper lady by showcasing her culinary achievements. She placed the remaining slices in a pail to save for Ned and her other nieces and nephews. She had a much better idea than pound cake.

By the time the men entered, her father was concluding his story of how his father-in-law reconsidered the courtship of a recently widowed Cherokee officer when he came back for

Miss Mary Meade after the war. How she became a mother to his children and gave him Anna.

Anna poured two strong cups of coffee and set them alongside a couple of bowls.

The men took their seats, and her father eyed the table. "Where is the pound cake?"

"I'm afraid I already promised it to Ned." She placed an earthen jar in the middle of the board. "But we have *ganache-ni*."

Father's shoulders squared. "Bring us the cake, daughter."

She made a show of hesitating. "Very well, though Ned will be disappointed. But first, we should offer our guest a serving of ganache. This would not be a proper visit to a Cherokee home, otherwise." Anna removed the lid of the cracked corn that had been cooked several hours before lye was added, then fermented, and reached for a spoon...but paused with her hand still in the air. She raised her eyebrow. "Unless, of course, the sergeant prefers cake."

There was no way Sergeant Edmonds could know that to refuse would insult both her and her father. Perhaps their visit would be over sooner than hoped. Anna held her breath.

And the sergeant held her gaze. "I would never dream of declining ganache."

He even pronounced the Cherokee word right. She tried not to deflate as she dipped up his serving and slid it over to him. Her normally stoic father pressed his lips together in what certainly appeared to be an effort to contain a smile. She passed him his serving with a quirk of her own lips—an irritated one —before returning to the hearth. She moved the skillet with the bean bread closer to the small orange flames.

"Now you know how I became a soldier," her father said over a slurp of coffee, "but you must tell us how you became one."

"I mentioned my father served in the Creek War. I have

two sisters—a twin who is married, and a younger one still at home. That left me to follow in my father's footsteps, although I never did envision myself as a soldier." The sergeant's spoon scraped his bowl. "This was delicious, Miss Walker."

Anna gave a nod and turned back to add a small scoop of lard to the skillet.

"What did you want to be?" her father asked.

Their guest gave a rueful laugh. "Actually...a missionary." His admission almost made Anna swivel her head again. "I've always been something of a peacemaker and good at languages. Unfortunately, I also needed some toughening up."

"So you enlisted in the Mounted Militia to come to Cherokee Territory."

"Only after I served in Florida. Last spring, in Captain Thomas Holland's Gainesville Dragoons."

Anna stiffened. He had fought against the Seminoles who simply wanted to keep their land like the Cherokees? That bean bread was frying up far too nice and golden brown. Rather than flipping it and adding a sweet sear with molasses as she normally would do, she reached for the salt crock.

Her father's fingers drummed the table. "Part of General Scott's campaign."

"His ill-fated campaign, yes." Was that regret that laced the sergeant's reply? Regret that heavy rain and disease had prevented the five thousand men sent to Florida from killing and capturing enough Seminoles?

Anna sprinkled a generous amount of salt over the bean bread as her father spoke again.

"The Seminoles absorbed a number of Creek refugees after the Red Stick War. They were fierce warriors." The old allegiance the Creeks had to the British would no doubt justify the 1836 campaign in her father's mind, as it would in the sergeant's.

Anna stood with her toe tapping and watched the bean bread turn dark brown.

The bench creaked as their guest shifted his considerable frame. "As well as the slaves they freed from sugar plantations, yes. Not to mention, they knew the lay of the land, and we did not."

"Edmonds..." Her father set down his cup with a clunk, as though something had just occurred to him. "Colonel Garrison Edmonds was your father?"

"That was him." Was it Anna's imagination, or did a hint of unease tinge Gage's reply?

"Ah, yes. His men were among the first over the defenses... once we Cherokees swam the river behind the Creek town of Tohopeka and broke the stalemate of Jackson's cannonade." A hint of laughter rumbled behind Father's statement.

"There is no doubt the Cherokee Regiment won the day. My father would be the first to credit that. It was why he wanted me to serve in the Mounted Militia—to help keep the peace for his former allies."

There it was again—that misguided notion that his presence here could do some good. Anna whirled from the hearth. "It's a little late for that, Sergeant Edmonds. Jackson has already failed us."

His eyebrows shot up. "Did I not hear you remind your friend at church that negotiations still hold out hope?"

"Temporary hope. We all know the army will eventually get what it wants."

He stiffened. "It's not what we want, Miss Walker. It's what the settlers want."

"And the government...which we know is one and the same."

"Anna." Her father's stern tone brought her up short. "Is the stew ready?"

The smell of something burning permeated the air. She

whisked around to flip the bean bread and remove the skillet from the flames. Then she transferred servings for the men onto plates. As she set it before them, she kept her chin up. "My apologies, but the stew is gone. We'll have to make do with yesterday's bean bread." While avoiding her father's glare, she made sure to give the sergeant the darkest piece. Let the Indian-killer choke on that.

He stared at the blackened square a moment before turning a smile up to her that made her stomach do somersaults. "Miss Walker, you can't know how happy this makes me. It's been so long since I've had bean bread."

She barely refrained from gaping at him. Was this man impossible to ruffle? "I hope it's just to your liking, then."

He broke off a corner and snagged a sample. His only reaction was a quick blink before he chewed and swallowed. "Delicious. In fact, I won't tell Aginisi that yours makes hers taste rather bland." He flashed her a grin and reached for his coffee.

Father's scowl promised an evening of discomfort. "My daughter, who is normally an excellent cook, is distracted today, Sergeant Edmonds. I trust you can forgive her. It's an honor to have a fine soldier such as yourself to share a meal with us."

"Please." The sergeant laid his hands on the table. "No apology is needed. You've both made me feel quite at home."

Anger seared her like a lightning strike. "But you're not home, Sergeant Edmonds. You're in *our* home. And having a Cherokee nurse who taught you the language and made you our foods does not make you Cherokee. If it did, you wouldn't presume to come here talking about protection and peace."

Finally, her words had the desired effect. At the same time her father growled her name, Sergeant Edmonds dropped his head. He sat for a moment and took a deep breath, then slowly unfolded his long frame and reached for the hat he'd laid on the bench beside him. "You're right. I've presumed on your hospitality. I will take my leave." He turned to her father and dipped his chin. "Thank you for the invitation and good conversation."

The shame on her father's face bled all the fight out of Anna. Her shoulders slumped, and she stepped forward. "Sergeant, please forgive—"

He held up a hand. "There's nothing to forgive. I would only say there's nothing I hope for more than that you should remain in your home...for many generations." He slid on his hat and crossed the floor. With his hand on the latch, he turned back. His gaze skittered to Anna's, then away. "And my grandfather married Aginisi. So she *was* family." He left the cabin, quietly closing the door behind him. His humble leave-taking censured her far more sharply than her father's words ever could. But even her father remained silent.

Anna stared down at the burned bean bread—her childish attempt to make a point—and sudden tears swam in her eyes. Her attempt to defend her father's people had instead brought him reproach. And perhaps worse, her bitter campaign against the army had hurt another good man...one she would probably now never get to know.

CHAPTER 5

$\mathcal{A}$ day shy of a week after his visit to the Walkers, the abrupt nature of his departure from their home still goaded Gage. How could he have handled it better? The question nagged at the back of his brain as he rode Colby alongside an army wagon driven by Assistant Quartermaster John Wood. Private Newton Perkins rode shotgun as they passed through an area known by the Cherokees as Etowah Mount, the settlement ruled by Chief Old Still. Perkins, whose stepfather owned the land they were establishing Fort Buffington on, had pointed out the native leader's river-bottom home and the racetrack for the fine horses bred by many mixed-blood Cherokees. Perkins said the thoroughbreds sometimes raced for a twenty-four-carat trophy, The Golden Horse, made by a native goldsmith.

They'd been to Canton to purchase enough supplies to plug the gap until the end-of-the-month delivery from New Echota arrived—salt, coffee, sugar, and bacon, for the most part. The likelihood that the scheduled shipment would include more corn to be taken to the mill might've been what jogged Gage's unease. Anna Walker's stricken countenance haunted him, blotting out even the bright late-October day as they rode along.

Over and over, he'd returned to the notion that he couldn't have done anything differently. He wouldn't force his company on anyone—least of all a young lady he admired. Neither could he have explained his sentiments any better to the Walkers. Given the situation her people faced, he couldn't blame Anna for her resentment. If only she would see he was on her side. Still, as he'd left, in the slump of her shoulders and the softening of her countenance, he'd dared to believe she'd begun to grasp his position. He'd hoped against hope that she might follow him onto the porch. But she hadn't.

And that left him questioning his mission here. Was she right? Was he just a cog in a machine rolling inevitably forward? Would this assignment end as futilely as the one in Florida? He couldn't believe that...or it was pointless. All pointless. And his debt to his father would forever go unpaid.

"What's goin' on over there?" Private Wood's question and the distant hum of voices and occasional shouts drew Gage from his introspection. In a vast field between the Alabama Road and the Etowah River, a crowd had gathered. On Old Still's land?

Private Perkins sat up straighter, answering Gage's unspoken question. "That's Hood's field. I forgot, today's the big match."

"What match?" Gage rode closer as Private Wood slowed the wagon with a creaking and jingling.

"Hickory Log Village versus Coosawattee." Perkins used the Cherokee term for the Etowah. "This is the game everyone waits for all year." At Private Wood's quick, frowning glance, Perkins clarified, "Stickball."

"Ah, yes." Gage craned his neck for a better view of the crowd surrounding the field. "My grandmother used to tell me how the braves played stickball in preparation for battle. Hopefully, this is just for fun."

"Yeah, although they take it just as seriously. May we stop a minute?" Private Perkins's face lit with boyish pleading.

At Gage's nod, Private Wood edged the team off the road and pulled up on the reins before Perkins continued.

"Before the game, the men go to the river and rub slippery elm or sassafras all over themselves. Makes them slicker than a greased pig to catch hold of." Perkins flashed a grin at their alarmed expressions. "For two hours, they battle to get the ball through those goals. Play doesn't stop even if bones are broken."

Gage's squinting glance sought doorframe-like poles erected at either end of the field. "No one seems to be on the field yet."

"First, they'll be drinking. Placing bets."

"Even with a hundred-dollar fine on both the buyer and seller?" Gage had heard from his superiors of the efforts of the leaders to staunch the flow of liquor in the Cherokee Nation.

"At events like this? Oh, yeah. A few years back, the rival chiefs bet a thousand dollars on the game. Someone is always designated to watch the knives and pocketbooks during the fun...though the women never drink."

"But they come watch this rough sport?" Private Wood gaped at him.

"Sure do." Private Perkins waved his hand. "There will be people hanging from trees all around the field for the best view. Wish we could stay." He pointed to clusters of people several hundred yards away. "Right now, it looks like they're starting off with a stalk shooting."

That needed no explanation, as men in fringed hunting shirts and buckskin trousers stained a rich tan from walnut juice lined up about a hundred-and-fifty yards from a thick bundle of cornstalks.

Some men still sported the moccasins, gorgets, and slit ears with dangling earrings of their ancestors, while others had adopted a more European style with frock coats and floppy hats or turbans.

Whatever their clothing, their lithe physiques and the ease with which they pulled back their longbows for practice shots made Gage glad he didn't have to face them in battle. Especially the tall Cherokee who whipped an arrow out of his quiver for the first official shot and sent it sailing dead center of the target, piercing through to the turkey feather fletching, much to the enthusiasm of the crowd. He wore his long hair clubbed back rather than cropped. Leggings rather than trousers. As he moved to the back of the line, he brushed close to a bonneted woman in a green calico dress.

"That was a good one. Points are awarded depending on the number of stalks the archer's arrow hits," Perkins was saying, but Gage's attention had strayed from the competitors to the couple, now speaking with their heads tilted close together. Could that be...?

His heart rate picked up. She wasn't his business.

A moment later, the man slid his hand down the woman's arm and twined his fingers with hers, drawing her toward a nearby oak with his longbow in his other hand. As she turned, her features became visible past the high brim of her bonnet. Anna.

Gage didn't stop to ponder why he was thinking about her by her given name. He just pressed his heels into Colby's flanks and started riding closer to the pair. Some instinctual protectiveness had taken control.

"Sergeant?" Private Wood's query trailed at his back.

Gage waved his hand. "You men proceed to the encampment. I'll be along shortly."

He didn't wait to see if they obeyed, but the rumble of wagon wheels a moment later vaguely registered, confirming they had. Gage focused on the archer who resembled the fierce braves his father had described fighting alongside at the Battle of Horseshoe Bend...before so many of the Cherokee people had Americanized in an effort to live peaceably among their white neighbors. He had Anna backed so far up against the tree, she had to keep herself upright with a hand on its trunk. Practically pinned. Heat raced along Gage's spine like a strike to a lightning rod.

"Haw." He gave a soft command to his stallion, and the horse scampered forward.

And none too soon. Foekiller—surely, the popular Cherokee name would suit one so confident with his stance and his bow—had swooped his head in low, and when Anna turned her face to one side, his hand came up to brace her jaw.

Gage sucked in a quick breath. "Miss Walker!" Thankfully, her proper title came out, though none too sweetly.

She jerked away, stumbling slightly to one side. Her face slackened with surprise as her admirer shot Gage a glare that could've melted the frost off the pumpkins.

"Sergeant Edmonds." Did he imagine it, or was that relief on her face? "What are you doing here? Did my father...?" Her tone wavered between panic and hope.

"He's fine. But I believe you are needed at the mill." Would that do?

Anna cast an anxious glance toward Foekiller, who moved closer to her and said in a tone almost too low for Gage to hear, "You're leaving? Before the game?"

Where the players competed without adequate clothing? There could be no way Mr. Walker would countenance that... not when he'd sacrificed so much for his daughter to have a proper upbringing. Gage nudged Colby nearer to Anna. "I'm going that way if you'd like to ride with me." He leaned a hand down toward her.

Foekiller smacked it out of the way. "You don't belong here, soldier boy." A string of colorful Cherokee that questioned Gage's parentage and manhood followed the pronouncement.

Acting as though he didn't understand, Gage merely extended his hand again. This time, Anna took it, and he pulled her onto the saddle in front of him before she could change her mind. Petticoats frothed like river rapids, and sassy striped stockings peeped out above black boots. Anna didn't seem to mind that she rode astride, as she made no move to cover her shapely limbs. Gage wheeled Colby toward the road and did not look back, though his shoulder blades tightened as he couldn't help but imagine an arrow piercing his back. He only slowed down when Hood's field was out of sight.

"Well." Anna released a heavy breath. "You've done it now."

"Interfered in your business again?" He braced himself for the onslaught of scolding.

"Well, there's that." Her rueful chuckle relaxed him a bit. She wasn't angry at him. He must have read her right.

"You seem to have a number of suitors." It wasn't hard to see why...especially when he cradled her soft curves so near. The sun glinted off her dark hair, worn in a low bun beneath her bonnet, and the scent of crisp cotton and something floral teased his nose. He forced his mind to the road with the black-eyed Susans and Queen Anne's lace abloom alongside. And slowed down. He didn't want to catch up to Wood and Perkins.

"And that one I actually wanted."

Gage stiffened. "You wanted him pawing at you?"

"He wasn't..." She turned partway around, then, as if noticing how close their faces were, faced forward abruptly. "I said I wanted the suitor, not to be pinned against a tree."

The protective surge ebbed, and once again, Gage relaxed. "Then I'm glad I happened along."

"What *are* you doing here?" She kept her hands on the front of the saddle and only angled her head a small degree this time. "Does my father really need me?"

"I'd accompanied two privates into Canton for supplies, so no, I don't come bearing any message from your father. But I can't imagine he'd want you in the midst of such an event."

"As you should know if your grandmother taught you anything, stickball is a time-honored Cherokee tradition." Indignation heated her reply as her chin lifted.

"For unmarried, unescorted, properly educated young women?" When she didn't reply, Gage added, "Does your father even know you were there?"

She blew out a little breath. "I told him I was going to Mrs. Campbell's. Which I did." She nodded ahead as a two-story white clapboard inn came into view. "That's where I left my horse."

Disappointment that their ride was almost over swept Gage and ought to have set all sorts of alarms off in his head. But the Anna Walker who rode ahead of him was not the same one he'd left in her cabin a week ago. Something had shifted. Thawed. So instead, he found himself saying, "Will you allow me to accompany you home?"

"I ought not to." She did turn then, twisting her pink lips into a pretty pout. "After all, you ruined my plans to ensnare Smoke Sanders."

"Ha." What a name. Foekiller suited the showoff better. "No apologies for that." The heat that spread in his chest at their banter could become addictive. So could that smile of hers.

"...and earned his ire. He's not an enemy you want to make."

"Let me worry about that." Given the tense climate they all found themselves in, he did not take her warning lightly, even though he lifted one shoulder in a gesture meant to ease her fears.

"You've also got Micah Thompson to watch out for. You're making enemies on all sides, Sergeant Edmonds." Real concern sparked in her dark eyes as she surveyed him.

"Seems I find myself in need of a friend. What about that ride?"

"I'll agree…" She wobbled, and he steadied her about her waist. How trim and slender she was under his gloved hand. With a sudden flush to her cheeks, she continued. "I'll agree because I treated you awfully when we last met. I owe you an apology, so I can hardly be angry at you for inserting yourself today. In fact, I owe you my thanks as well as an apology. It seems Smoke Sanders was a little more interested than I thought."

And so was he. As evidenced by the cresting of warmth in his chest when her small hand closed over his. "No thanks or apologies necessary. I'd just like us to start over, Miss Walker, if that's all right by you."

"Start what over?" They'd pulled up in front of the Campbell Inn, with its rocking chair-lined verandas and Sweet Williams nodding in flowerboxes. When Anna turned to eye him again, Gage's breath stuck in his throat.

Whatever you want to start. The words were on the tip of his tongue, but thankfully, what he managed to get out sounded a lot more sensible. "How about a tour of the mill?"

~

The relief on Joshua Walker's face when Gage rode with Anna into the yard reassured him he'd done right by bringing her home. The older man greeted them from the stoop of the mill. "How was your visit with Mrs. Campbell?" he asked his daughter as she dismounted.

"Very nice, Edoda." She led her mare closer and kissed his cheek. "Sergeant Edmonds happened to be passing this way and offered to accompany me home."

"We thank you, Sergeant." Joshua's sincere gaze as he shook Gage's hand hinted that he'd been well aware of the stickball game and concerned about its proximity to the inn. Did he also know about Smoke...Smokes? Foekiller? "Will you stay to supper? We have plenty of stew this time." He did not so much as crack a smile.

Before Gage could reply, Anna spoke for him. "Sergeant Edmonds was just telling me how much he'd like a tour of the mill. It seems he is fascinated by gears and pulleys and such." Her tone suggested she suspected him of coming up with excuses to be near her.

He wasted no time in justifying his interest. "I have my engineering degree, so naturally, anything mechanical interests me."

She cocked her head. "Then why are you in the army?"

"To honor my father and serve my grandmother's people... remember?" Had she not listened to anything he'd said to her father on his last visit? Perhaps his fascination with her *was* entirely one-sided. "The plan is to help open the Southern frontier with roads and bridges."

"No doubt that will come in handy after all the original inhabitants are forced out."

Gage stiffened. Why offer an apology and then continue to spar? Then he noted the teasing flash to her eyes. Oh, this was a lively one. He sought a quick retort but delivered it with a grin. "My plan clearly doesn't stand a chance against a foe such as yourself, Miss Walker."

Her dimple winked at him. "Well...then you know not to return unless you wish to engage in full-out battle."

Was that a challenge? Gage's grin widened. "I will deliver our next corn shipment under a flag of truce, miss."

"Fine. Although I have yet to be convinced of your personal motivations."

Joshua Walker looked between the two of them with his eyebrows slowly inching upward. Then he gestured to the hitching post. "Come, Sergeant. Tie off your horse, and I will show you the workings before I shut her down for the day."

After he did as his host suggested, Gage couldn't resist a glance over his shoulder. Rather than following him into the mill as he'd hoped, Anna led her mare toward the stable. She caught his glance and failed to smother a smirk in time. Would she really welcome his return?

Inside the building, Joshua showed Gage more than he'd seen upon his initial visit, including the cranes and bails used to lift the massive runner stones from their casings so steel picks could be used to dress the surfaces to keep them sharp for grinding. In the basement, Gage examined the pit wheel mounted on the same axle as the waterwheel, which powered the smaller wallower on a driveshaft that ran from the bottom to the top of the building. Joshua explained that the system ensured that the main shaft turned faster than the waterwheel, which typically rotated about ten revolutions per minute.

As they walked along the raceway to the sluice gate and Anna's father spoke of previous years of flooding and drought and innovative ways they'd managed to continue providing meal for the community, his face shone with pride. The music of the shoals underscored his words in a natural symphony. This was not man who sounded as though he had any intention of leaving.

Gage stood for a moment watching the stream play and rubbing his jaw. "Mr. Walker, what will you do if Chief Ross is unsuccessful in securing your land?"

Joshua's expression sobered. "There are those who say now that he is negotiating to hold onto at least a portion of it. I do not believe it is so. Our head chief, Rising Fawn, hears directly from those in Washington. The men in power believe this land was won from Britain. They do not consider who was here before the English. He says we must prepare to go."

Gage's stomach tightened. "Will you accept the money the government offers for improvements on your land, then?"

The man made a rumbling sound. "Hm. Some have advised me to do so. To take the money and clear out before things get worse. Chief George Welch owned the mill on Settingdown Creek, valued by the government at over seven hundred dollars. This year, Jacob Scudder bought it from the man who drew the property in the lottery for two hundred and fifty."

"We both know what you get would never be enough for a fair restart in Oklahoma—not to mention giving up your family land. That means more than you can put a price on." Gage's ire deepened his reply. "This is wrong—injustice in its lowest form."

Joshua turned and studied him for a long moment. He was obviously a man to whom silence was a friend, a giver of gifts. Gifts such as introspection, wisdom, and discretion. "You are a rare white man, Sergeant Edmonds. I am glad we have a friend in you."

"You do. I just wish I knew what any of us could do." Gage shook his head.

"Like my chiefs, I make my own quiet preparations."

What did that mean? The vagueness of the statement did not invite exploration, but Joshua's direct gaze also excluded dishonesty. Gage sighed. Whatever the man had planned, how effective could it be against such powerful forces? "If there is anything I can do to aid you..."

"I will bear that in mind." The speculative gleam in Joshua Walker's eye as he led Gage back to the mill left a lasting question in his mind.

CHAPTER 6

She was a fool. No, she was worse than a fool. She was a coward.

Anna berated herself as she stomped up the path that followed Walker Creek at the end of the first week of November. She made no effort at stealth in the crunchy fallen leaves and fairly growled at the late-afternoon sun dancing through colorful tree limbs. When the big canvas foraging sack she'd looped over her shoulder caught on a briar, she jerked it free without breaking her stride toward the stand of willows where she'd seen the most honeysuckle over the summer.

Ever since Gage Edmonds had brought her home from the stickball match, she'd been unable to rid her mind of him. Like chaff in grain. Like weevils in flour.

The first sign of trouble ought to have been her lack of ire that the sergeant ambushed her chances of securing Smoke Sanders's interest. Never mind the fact that the man's intentions might have been of a questionable nature. That was beside the point. The sergeant riding in like a conquering knight to her rescue when he had not been invited, when he had no reason to be at Hood's field, was exactly what she would have expected from a member of the mounted militia. Stranger still was the relief that had swept her at his appearance...relief she'd been unable to hide...obviously.

Her trust had not been misplaced. He'd been a perfect gentleman as she'd ridden before him, keeping her secure while retaining a respectful distance. But the touch of his gloved hand and the teasing rumble of his voice did strange things to her middle and made ganache-ni of her mind, for she'd ended up flirting with the man. Practically dared him to come back. Where had that come from?

Then a week passed. Every day, she increasingly reproached herself, for each time a wagon rumbled up to the mill, she rushed to the Dutch door with her heart in her throat, only to be disappointed when another farmer in a floppy hat unloaded his corn.

Anna reached the stand of willows near a small shoals of the creek. Yellowing leaves fell among the twisting vines and created a soft carpet on the forest floor. The burbling of water over a cluster of smooth stones behind her underscored the rustle of wind through the trees as she identified a long, hearty vine and shook it to reveal its path. Moving up the bank, she traced the creeper to its termination in a branch above her head and began to untwine the length, careful not to break it. She coiled it around her arm as she worked.

Now that the sap had dropped, the vines that often grew to lengths of over twenty feet would make an excellent basket. But her errand was just an excuse...for Gage Edmonds had finally arrived that morning. That was when her foolishness had turned into cowardice. The sight of him sitting tall and strong on the wagon seat had turned her insides to jelly, and she'd darted away with some excuse about checking on the cabbage leaves she was drying. Her father's perplexed look had followed her out the back door.

Only, she hadn't gone to check on cabbage leaves. She'd

stood outside the mill to hear the conversation. Agidoda had told Gage they were so backed up grinding the last corn of the harvest that it might be best if he returned at the end of the day, to which he'd agreed...after asking about her. Her father had indicated she had not gone far and would surely wish to say hello when Gage returned. Which she did. But what could she say after that?

There was no point in conversing with Gage Edmonds and even less justification for the butterflies in her stomach. Their paths diverged. How could her father forget? How could she?

At last, Anna traced the honeysuckle vine to its root. She removed her bone-handled knife from its beaded sheath around her neck and cut the end. Carefully, she tucked the coil into her sack. She took a deep breath and forced her racing thoughts to slow, to align with the cadence of nature around her. She located another promising vine and repeated the harvesting process.

By the time she collected half a dozen coils in her bag, leaving the oldest and the youngest vines in the vicinity to replenish, her heart beat steadily, and the sun's tangerine glow had dimmed to the color of buttery silk. A mourning dove called from a nearby branch, and tiny animal paws scampered to their burrows. It was time to return home and heat the succotash. Father would be hungry. No doubt, so would Ned, whom she'd left assisting him when she'd skedaddled the second time under Agidoda's disapproving frown. Why did he care if she greeted the sergeant? Wasn't it Father who believed they would be forced to leave?

No matter. By the time she returned, Gage Edmonds was the one who would be gone. And when she encountered him next, she would have mastery over this silly feminine response of hers.

Anna set out for home, this time with steps that respected the hush of twilight. Her chest seemed to cave in on her heart.

She loved this land. It was the only place she belonged. She'd heard Oklahoma was flat, treeless. How could one live without the shelter of the giants of the forest, the dips of the land that promised and then revealed new secrets within each fold? The voice of the dancing creek? The breathtaking sunsets over the hills?

The murmur of voices ahead, furtive in their volume and tension, slowed her pace. She approached a turn in the trail with caution, skirting behind a massive oak. Two young Cherokee men she didn't recognize crouched beside a boulder that marked a bend in the creek. They consulted a paper, then each other. Finally, one reached in his bandolier bag and pulled out something that glinted in the dimming light. Some sort of tool. He crouched before the boulder, his boots splashing in water that lapped the pebbled shore, while the other man appeared to stand watch, glancing up and down the trail.

Anna sank behind the tree, and the lookout stiffened, frowning in her direction. Did he see her? Her heartrate sped.

At the same moment, a touch to her shoulder caused her to suck in a breath. Thick, warm fingers covered her mouth as she turned—right into Gage Edmond's broad chest. Her eyes went wide. What was he doing here?

Keeping one hand over her mouth, he raised the first finger of the other to his lips. Then he tipped his head toward the men. Wherever he had come from, he, too, had surmised they were looking for more than fish. Or gold.

The chink of metal against stone drew her attention back to the creek side. When Anna leaned to peer that direction again, Gage braced her with both hands to her shoulders. Only her foraging bag containing its coils of springy vine separated her from the warmth of his body. He held her secure while she ascertained that the one man was carving something on the boulder.

She turned and raised her brows. Then pointed around the tree.

Gage frowned and shook his head.

This was ridiculous. This was her father's land. Why were they hiding and peeking as though there was some danger? She had every right to march over there and demand to know what those men were doing.

As if reading her thoughts, Gage slid back one side of his overcoat, and his hand drifted to the pistol he wore on his belt. Another shake of his head. He didn't wish to stumble into something sensitive and invite a confrontation. A wise decision, given the current state of affairs in Cherokee County. Anna flattened her mouth but nodded. His fingers brushed her arm...a thanks for her understanding. But his touch imparted much more than gratefulness, as it sent a tingle all the way up to her shoulder.

She flattened herself against the tree so he would put some space between them and waited until the tapping ended. Another glance past rough bark revealed that the lookout stood over the stone carver as if to approve his work. A few words in Cherokee were exchanged. The first man rose as the second produced the paper again. They spoke, pointed upstream, then almost noiselessly crossed the creek, leaping like young stags from rock to rock until they crested the far bank.

At last, Anna drew a deep breath. She didn't wait for Gage to speak but rather darted over to the rock and stood staring at the new engraving there.

He came and loomed behind her, a palpable presence in the dusk. "What does it mean?"

Anna knelt and traced the hollow plus symbol with her finger. "A crossing of paths, I think. But why mark it here?"

"Perhaps your father will know."

She rose and found herself all too close to him again. Anna stepped back. "Does he know *you're* here?"

Gage's green eyes shifted away from hers. "He seemed concerned that you had been gone for some time, so I came to check on you while he closed up the mill and Ned loaded my wagon."

"Very kind of you."

Her wry tone drew his gaze back. "And fortuitous, it would seem, with two strangers sneaking about."

Anna sniffed. "They were no danger to me. As you said, Agidoda likely knows they were here. Although..." She surveyed the symbol again. "I can't imagine why they're making a map on our land."

"A map? Is that what this is?" His brow furrowed.

She shrugged as she turned to head toward home. "Our people have long left symbols on the land, from rocks to trees. Saddle trees, pull trees, knee trees. But mostly to give direction to villages, trails, and waterways. There would be no need for such here."

Gage remained silent as if deep in thought while he followed her along the path.

Finally, she asked, "Something troubling you?"

Her glance over her shoulder revealed a lifting of his frown. "No...yes. Just thinking about something your father said. And also, to be honest, it wasn't your father's concern so much as mine that made me seek you out, Miss Anna...if I may call you that."

She stiffened at the sudden familiarity of her name on his lips but then played off her discomfort with a chuckle. "Does that mean I should call you 'Mr. Gage'? 'Sergeant Gage'? Either sounds rather awkward."

"Just 'Gage' will do."

The sobriety in his tone shut off her humor quick as the sluice gate cutting off the raceway flow. He couldn't really expect her to call him by his Christian name, could he? That implied friendship, trust...a future of some sort.

Once again as if reading her mind, he came back with an almost immediate response. "'Sergeant' seems so formal. And it calls to mind an unpleasant aspect of our relationship."

She paused where the trail emptied into the field in view of the mill complex. Asters floated like white clouds hovering low over the ground, late fingers of sunlight brushing the goldenrod with liquid fire while shadows deepened the long grasses to the color of moss-slicked rocks. Crickets chirped their trilling goodnight.

Anna pressed her lips together a moment before replying, taking in the beauty which contrasted with the sudden ache in her heart. "Nevertheless, an undeniable one." An impossible one.

He pulled his shoulders back and gazed at her with earnest sincerity. "Miss Anna...I would wish you to see me as a man, not a soldier. A friend, not an enemy. I thought we had made progress toward that...had begun to understand each other. But I couldn't help but feel you were avoiding me today. I'd like to know why."

"Why?" The word quivered like a slender pin oak leaf in a stiff wind. Panic soared. She couldn't tell him why.

He drew in and heaved out a breath. "Or perhaps simply tell me if you would prefer I not come back."

Not come back? No, oh, no. Before Anna could grapple with words, a movement inside the wavy glass of the mill's window caught her eye. She stood straighter. "Did you not say my father had shut up the mill?"

"He should have by now, yes." Gage's bemused reply reflected his confusion over the sudden shift in topic.

"Then why is someone in there?" She squinted for a sharper view across the darkening clearing. "The back door is ajar." Anna took off without looking to see if Gage followed. Something was wrong.

~

That girl was fast! "Anna!" Gage tried to slow her without calling too loudly, but she flitted over the field like a moth, impossible to catch.

He followed her through the back door of the mill, though his boots on the wooden floor prevented the stealth her moccasins afforded her. That entrance lay on the side of the building farthest from the waterwheel, which now sat motionless, the flow from the raceway cut off. And stealth they needed, for a hatchet blow to the board next to the doorjamb testified that someone had broken in and reached inside to lift the latch —an easier point of entry than the front door visible from the yard and cabin and secured with a wide timber bolt.

She darted around the platform that held the two giant sets of millstones. Before Gage could urge the same caution he had in the forest, she burst out. "Hey! What are you doing?"

Gage rounded the corner just as Anna flew at a man with his hat worn low and a bandana covering the bottom half of his face. A man who held a knife in one hand while he grasped the thickly woven canvas belt that carried the scoops of grain from the basement to the attic in the other. A knife! What was Anna doing?

Reaching for her own knife that hung at her neck!

"Stop!" His strangled cry rang out a second before the man released the belt to shove Anna, sending her toppling into a table against the wall. Gage's warning drew the man's attention. He flung the weapon. Gage ducked. Pain sliced through his shoulder, but the heavy blade clattered to the platform behind him.

He charged. The intruder ripped the wooden lever off the grain shoot at his side. As momentum carried Gage forward, the man raised his improvised weapon and brought it down over Gage's head. Darkness and showers of stars rained into his vision. His arms closed ineffectively around his opponent—loosely enough for the man to slip free and dart for the back door. Gage staggered to his knees.

"Gage!"

At Anna's horrified cry, he squeezed his eyes shut in an effort to clear his vision. Then opened them. He had to check on her. Holding onto the overturned table, Anna struggled upright. He pushed off the floor himself and took one step toward her before everything went black.

CHAPTER 7

Her heart thumping hard as the waterwheel when it was in operation, Anna scrabbled with the smooth-worn timber that bolted the front entrance of the mill. She hefted its cumbersome length aside and shoved open the door, yelling for her father at the same moment horse hooves pounded the packed-dirt clearing.

Agidoda must have already heard the commotion. He burst from the cabin with his musket in hand—one he'd managed to hide when soldiers had come through earlier that year, collecting the firearms of their people. As Anna ran toward him, he leveled the gun and sighted the intruder, only for him to round the bend. Agidoda's shot into the trees warned the man not to return. It also let him know they were armed. There would be more trouble from that.

Anna's concern remained on the fallen man in the mill. "Father!" She grabbed his arm. "Come. Sergeant Edmonds is injured."

"What happened?" Agidoda rushed with her across the yard.

"We were coming back from gathering honeysuckle vines

when I saw someone in the mill. They'd broken in the back door. We found a man cutting the belt."

Her father paused on the stoop and lifted his hand to her forehead, where the table must have left a mark. "You're hurt."

"'Tis nothing." She tugged him inside. "He threw his knife at Gage, then hit him over the head." She drew Agidoda to the sergeant's side. Still out cold. The knot swelling on Gage's temple and the scarlet blood seeping through his shirt and coat sleeve wrung her heart with dismay and fired her nerves with panic. How serious were his injuries? Some never awakened from a blow to the head.

After propping his musket against the toll booth, Father lightly smacked the side of the sergeant's face. Only a soft moan gave answer. Father pried open one of Gage's eyelids and peered at the pupil. He made a sound she didn't like. "We need to get him to the house. Run and fetch your brother."

Anna gathered her skirts close and hastened down the road to her half sibling's cabin. She found Crow outside splitting wood, forehead glistening along the line of his close-cropped black hair and muslin shirtsleeves rolled up. She gripped his muscled forearm as soon as he set down his ax. "There's been an accident. We need you."

He allowed her to pull him along without protest, but as she spilled the story, his dark brows lowered. He stopped in the mill yard. "You want me to aid a soldier?"

"Yes. I know how it sounds, but he was helping us. It's my fault he was attacked." She should have listened when Gage called her rather than running headlong into trouble as her fiery nature made her apt to do. Any lasting injury would be on her.

"This is the man who defended you against Thompson?" Apparently, Agidoda had told Crow of the confrontation over the corn toll. Of course he had. The whole family would be told, in order to be on alert.

"It was. Sergeant Edmonds. And I think this was Isaiah Thompson again today, though I barely got a glimpse of him before he flung me across the room and Gage charged him. Most of his face was covered."

Crow's expression darkened to the consistency of a thundercloud. He strode into the mill, Anna right behind him. Gage remained unconscious, only mumbling slightly as her father and brother both took a side and maneuvered him across the clearing and onto a quilt she hastily folded before the fire in the cabin. They worked in silence to strip him of his coat and shirt while Anna tied on her apron and turned to her box of herbs, fortifying herself with a deep breath and a prayer. Then she set to measuring and mixing as the women of her family had taught her. Goldenseal root for the inflammation from the blow. A poultice of ground sweetgum inner bark, heal-all, and yarrow leaves for the knife wound. How bad was it?

She turned to find her father holding a clean cloth over the sergeant's upper arm while her brother stood over them, still frowning. To be fair, he frowned most of the time lately. Understandably so. Anna did her best not to dwell on the well-defined planes and muscles of the sergeant's upper body as she drew near with her healing concoction. First, she needed to determine if stitches would be necessary. "I need more light."

Agidoda moved back to let Anna take his place. He stirred up the fire. Crow crisscrossed the cabin, opening windows and lighting the whale oil lamp using fatwood held in the flames their father had coaxed to life.

Release on the pressure of the wound caused another surge of blood, which Anna quickly mopped up, but she let out a little breath. "A glancing wound only. No stitches should be needed, but it will need to be cleaned well." She dabbed and peered closer for any particles of fabric. "Then I think some goldenseal as well as the poultice."

Agidoda *hmm*ed above her. "The knot on the head concerns me more...and how long he's been out."

Anna bit her lip when she surveyed the purpling lump above Gage's left eyebrow. "He was hit hard."

Crow plunked the oil lamp on the table and folded his arms over his sturdy chest. "I do not understand so much *concern* from both of you. Why was Anna with this *yu-ne-ga* at all?" Crow used the Cherokee term for *white man* for all settlers— generally, in a tone one reserved for explicates.

Before she could protest that she was sitting right before him, their father answered. "Your sister was gone overlong harvesting in the forest. The sergeant shares my concern for her safety with men like the Thompsons about...and well-placed it was."

"Not just with them." She secured the strip of cloth around Gage's arm and stood. "There were strange men in the forest. I almost walked up on them before Sergeant Edmonds found me."

Uncrossing his arms, Crow looked between them. "Doing what?"

Anna reached for the cast-iron kettle that hung to one side of the fireplace. She unhooked it with a cloth wrapped around her hand and poured some boiled water into a basin. "Carving a symbol onto a boulder by the creek." She faced her father. "Any idea why?"

Agidoda pressed his lips together and studied the sergeant as though to ensure Gage remained unconscious before he answered. "They were men from my village...Red Bank."

"All the way over here?" Anna gasped. "For what purpose?"

Agidoda hesitated again, then released a heavy sigh. "Reports from Washington are that Ross will not succeed. We are laying our own plans."

"To do what?"

"To secure our valuables so we may return for them after the resettlement."

Her mouth dropped open. "Along Walker Creek?" She knew what *valuables* meant. Gold. The Cherokees had been mining it for years before the arrival of the white settlers, especially at the hugely profitable Sixes Mine southwest of Canton.

Her father gave a somber nod.

"But how...why...?" She couldn't complete her sentence. If they were all gone, someone else would own this land, operate this mill. Wouldn't the newcomers find any hidden treasure before her people got the chance to return and reclaim it?

Agidoda tipped his head toward Gage. "The sergeant is part of my plan."

"But how can Gage do anything about it?" She only realized she had spoken his first name aloud when her brother raised his eyebrow.

Father didn't react. His stare into the fire told her he was focused inward, wrestling with something. Something that made her stomach hollow out like the gourds rattling over her garden. "As your husband, he could ensure you keep the land."

As her...husband? "No..."

Dormant pain that she'd managed to contain since childhood, deep down, roared upward, singeing the air from her lungs and further protest from her lips.

Anna staggered back a step. Her calves contacted the bench, and she collapsed onto it, sloshing water from the basin onto her apron. How could her father ever consider such a thing? Such a...betrayal? The one person who had always ensured she had a place to belong...didn't want her? Would leave her behind?

~

he anguish in Anna's one-word response cut through Gage's stupor, though he'd only grasped bits and pieces of the conversation prior as he swam to consciousness. Her father may as well have suggested she throw herself on a funeral pyre. Such an emphatic rejection might sting his masculine pride, but could he blame her? Was her father really suggesting a marriage of convenience, or were his wits more addled than Gage feared?

Only Gage himself could release her from this impossible situation. And he must do so immediately.

Despite the nausea causing his stomach to pitch and the room to tilt as though he was aboard a ship tossed in high seas, he forced his eyes open. He moaned low in his throat, signaling his return to alertness. He'd been moved to their cabin—presumably by Joshua Walker and the disapproving younger man who must be his son. How shameful. A single blow had cut him down like wheat under a scythe. How could he ever show his mettle as a soldier if he couldn't best a solitary foe?

Almost instantly, Anna was at his side, her concerned gaze sweeping him before she tossed a near-panicked glance at her relatives—clearly warning them to cease the discussion. She set a basin at his side. "How do you feel?"

That her compassion flowed alongside her distress credited her good character—indeed, showed her to be the type of woman he'd seek to wed, were he in the market. *Was* he in the market? No. Not until he proved himself on this assignment. And right now, that meant removing a burden—himself—from her. Between the embarrassment of his failure and her understandable horror at the notion of being shackled to an ineffectual white soldier, he couldn't beat a quick enough retreat.

"Well enough to get off your floor." Gage levered himself upright, but the room spun so fast, he stopped with a short intake of breath.

"Please wait." Was that moisture glistening in her eyes, or just the fire reflecting off her dark pupils? She laid an entreating hand on his chest—his *bare* chest—before jerking it back as his downward glance brought awareness to her mind and fetching color to her cheeks. "You risk injuring yourself further if you leave too soon. Besides, I need to tend your wounds."

Still, he hesitated. "I can have them taken care of at camp." Rather, take care of them himself, though he'd no intention of telling her that. They'd yet to receive a doctor at their post.

Anna gestured to two smaller bowls beside her, next to a short stack of linens. "I already have the poultices prepared. See? Our local herbs will help you heal faster than any of your white man's medicine."

"Which is mostly firewater," Joshua put in. His wry tone indicated his disapproval.

Gage submitted with a brief nod. He would not spurn their hospitality.

The younger man's fierce expression lingered as he gave a grunt of what sounded like disgust.

"Crow...let us speak outside." Joshua gestured to the door, and his son followed him onto the porch. They closed the door behind them, leaving Gage and Anna alone with only the measured but intense cadence of murmured male conversation carrying above the popping of the fire, the words indistinguishable. Was the man trying to convince his son of the rightness of his far-fetched plan? Somehow, for him to hold such hopes of success, he must have read how intriguing Gage found Anna. Or maybe he was just that desperate to save his legacy and spare his youngest child the pain of suffering and loss.

If Anna had indicated any willingness...

His chest squeezed. But as Gage swung his gaze to hers, something akin to panic flashed in the depths of her eyes. For her father to conceive of forcing her to wed a practical stranger...a white man? Whom she so clearly did not trust?

It was best that Gage stay far away.

But what could he say to ease her discomfort as she dipped a cloth into the basin of water and leaned forward to dab it over the cut on his arm? His breath whistled in as the fabric contacted his jagged skin, and a trickle of pink liquid ran down his bicep. She quickly wiped it away.

"I'm sorry." Her lashes fluttered upward for a brief glance. "We must ensure no debris remains in the cut."

"I'm the one who is sorry...to put you in such a position. I should have seen that coming."

She blinked at him. "Guessed he would tear the lever off the shoot and hit you over the head with it? No. It is I who was reckless. In the field as in the forest, you tried to call me back, but ever heedless, I ran straight into trouble."

"You were only trying to defend your property. Had a man done as you did, he would be called brave, not reckless."

Anna's lips parted as she stopped and stared at him a moment. Then she gave her head the barest shake. "I'm only glad he did not do more damage, and that was thanks to you. I shudder to think what might have happened had you not been there."

"Me, too, though I'm in no position to accept thanks." A soft groan escaped as Gage pressed his fingers to his throbbing head—on the other side from the ever-tightening knot. "It seems I'm accomplished at letting bad guys get away."

"What do you mean?" Anna's forehead creased. She lowered the cloth into the bowl of water and wrung it out.

"Just something that happened in Florida..." The blow must have addled his head. Otherwise, he wouldn't be speaking of the failure that had launched him on the path that led him here. Certainly not to her.

"In the Seminole War?"

He nodded, but the movement—or the memory—made bile rise in his throat, and he struggled up on his good arm, facing Anna, lest he further shame himself by casting up his accounts in front of her. He clenched his eyelids shut.

"Easy." She steadied him, her gaze concerned enough to be sensed even as he drew quick breaths and willed his stomach to settle. "Perhaps you need a drink of water."

"I'm fine." He didn't dare add anything to swirling mixture in his midsection.

"Then here…"

The cool cloth gently contacted the knot on his head, and Gage opened his eyes. "That does help. Thank you."

"The bad guys were Seminoles, weren't they?"

Gage sighed. He'd hoped he'd diverted her from digging in his past, but the way her lips pressed together required an explanation, lest he earn her further displeasure. "Yes. I told you I served with the Gainesville Dragoons in the spring of '36."

She gave a nod, her gaze wary, as she continued holding the cloth to his temple.

"The Seminoles had destroyed most sugar plantations and freed the slaves in the area of Florida where we were deployed. They knew the land. We didn't. We couldn't pin them down. Then finally one day, a small detachment I was with tracked several young warriors to a cabin on a plantation. Three of our men covered the front while I went with our Seminole scout to the forest behind it. More of a swamp, really." He shuddered as memories of muck, snakes, and gators surfaced from the hazy pool of memory.

Anna lowered the cloth. "Was this when you saw action for the first time?"

"No." He met her gaze, then looked away. "Just as the dragoons closed in at the front of the cabin, a panther screamed nearby. It threw the soldiers into enough confusion for the youths to escape out a back door…and join the scout a few hundred yards from me before slipping off into the trees."

She let out a little gasp. "He had given the scream."

"Yes." Gage dared to glance at her again. Speculation had replaced wariness as she nibbled her lower lip and frowned.

"You saw them...and you let them go?"

"I was close enough to see that they were not much more than boys."

Understanding dawned in her eyes. "Boys who were brave enough to fight for their land and help others gain freedom."

He dipped his head just enough to acknowledge her observation. "Yet that was no excuse for shirking my military duty. At least, not for my father."

"Surely, he forgave you once you explained."

Gage held back a grimace at the memory of his father's cold silence, his polite but marked withdrawal, the most painful weapon of his disapproval—a tactic that could not be argued with or outmaneuvered. "It was very important to Father that our family's loyalty to our country be beyond dispute."

"Why? You said he served with distinction in the War of 1812."

"He did...but in his mind, rumors and questions lingered. To have a son return with accolades would have cleared them up for good."

"Rumors and questions from whom?" Anna cocked her head, clearly confused by his partial explanation.

Gage heaved a deep breath and expelled the truth the Edmonds never spoke of. "From those who had heard portions of the true story, which was that my grandfather was a Loyalist who fought with the British during the Revolution...and then retreated to Cherokee Territory to hide." At least Anna was unlikely to judge him, given the fact that her people had fought alongside the British during the Revolution.

Her brows rose as she sat back on her heels. "Where he

started the trading post and met the woman who became your Cherokee grandmother." She remembered what he had told her that first Sunday he'd come to visit and she'd tried to scare him off with bad cooking. At least she'd been listening.

"That's right. Add to that the fact that the Seminoles had absorbed not only freed slaves but also the Creek Indians who had fled rather than be removed after the War of 1812. Father considered them his bitter enemy...and the enemy of your people. So when the chance came to redeem myself in Cherokee Territory, I took it."

"To please him." Anna bunched the damp cloth and laid it beside the water, apparently forgotten.

"To honor his memory." The last of his energy seemed to seep out with the words, and Gage eased himself back onto the floor, folding the hand of his good arm over his middle.

"His...memory?" Her query came out whisper-soft.

He might as well admit the worst of his guilt. "My father died of the swamp fever I brought home to him." He closed his eyes and kept them closed even when she gave a soft gasp.

"Oh, Sergeant." She pressed her hand briefly on his arm. "Surely, you cannot blame yourself."

Gage turned his head and looked at her levelly. "Who else?"

"You are trying to redeem yourself in his estimation, but he is gone." Sorrow pooled in her eyes.

"I told you because I wanted you to understand why I have to serve honorably this time. I know he's gone. This is something I have to do for me." He waited until she gave a nod, though she didn't appear convinced. It was enough for now. "And for you. So...today at the mill...you think it was Thompson? The older one?"

"Isaiah. Yes, although I cannot say for sure." She frowned in concentration. "He did have the man's bearing and eyes."

"Would you like me to pay him a visit with a small company

of mounties? Ask a few questions? Just let him know we're onto him?"

"No. Please don't." In what was clearly an impulsive gesture, she pressed her hand over his.

The touch was no doubt intended to convey the urgency of her discouragement, but before Gage thought it through, his hand flipped over, and he entangled his fingers in hers. "But this has to stop. I can't rest easy if you and your family are in danger." If he was to absent himself from the mill, he at least needed to know the local bullies would bring no more trouble upon the Walkers.

Anna's breath shuddered in softly, and she held it a moment while her fingers jerked reflexively against his—as if she wanted to hold on but feared to. Feared to trust him, despite the fact that he had just laid himself bare. Then, in a gesture that incited an ache in his chest, she slid her hand from his and reached for the cloth. "There is no need. No damage was done."

Gage couldn't stop himself from arguing. "This time. What if you hadn't seen him when you did? What if he had cut that belt in multiple places, as he probably intended to do? How long would that have put you out of commission?"

"It is not your problem. My father and brother will handle it." She tilted her dark head toward the door, from the other side of which still came voices.

Of course. How self-focused to have believed the discussion between the men centered on him. No doubt, they were formulating a plan to safeguard the mill with the help of their kinsmen, as they had done successfully for decades. The truth was, Anna didn't need him. His presence only complicated matters. "Until there's a confrontation between the whites and the Cherokees here."

Had he spoken his thought aloud? Anna's startled glance confirmed he had.

But rather than respond, she squeezed more water over the

wound on his arm, keeping the extra cloth below. "Now you must hold still while I pack in some goldenseal. It may sting a bit."

Business it was, then. Before he showed any sign of distress over her dressing a simple cut, he'd be escorted from camp with bells, whistles, and tin cans as Private Pettyjohn had been at New Echota, when the boy had stolen thirty dollars from a fellow soldier. Gage didn't move a muscle while Anna dabbed a chunky paste in the valley of his rent flesh. He allowed himself to relax a bit while she smoothed dampened plant material from the other bowl onto one side of a strip of cloth which she then bound around his arm.

"Keep this in place until morning. It would be best if you come back for me to tend it." The glance she flicked his way hinted at something deeper beneath the suggestion...a fear that he actually would?

Gage waved the hand of his uninjured arm in a dismissive gesture. "No need."

"Then I'll send some of the poultice with you. Add a bit of boiled water tomorrow and apply it to a clean cloth as you saw me do. *Ha-wa*?"

He nodded. "All right." Her lack of argument only confirmed that he was right to sever ties. But the idea of doing so, of possibly never seeing her again just when she had begun to lower her guard and allow him to glimpse something beautiful, something promising, left him with an ache in his middle that no food or herb was likely to quench.

CHAPTER 8

Four days after the intruder wounded Gage, Anna opened the mill for the day armed with her broom. She attacked the dust and chaff that coated the rough-hewn floors with enough vigor to send Ned into a sneezing fit. The debris she inhaled coated her own nostrils, but she whisked each corner and cranny with the vigor of a chimney sweep.

Every effort to talk to her father about his outlandish suggestion had only resulted in him saying he wanted to spare her leaving her home...to provide her with the security of the legacy their family had built here. He didn't seem to understand that without her people, she had no legacy. The sense of abandonment grew with every futile conversation, yet she couldn't bring herself to voice how his suggestion resurrected the rejection she'd faced in her youth.

As for Gage, she'd given up on trying to make heads or tails of his words and actions. His goal of opening up the Southern lands for settlement was at odds with her very existence. But then the concern he'd expressed for the safety and future of her family had settled in her heart with the weight of sincerity. And his touch...

She shivered with a chill that had naught to do with the frosty November morning. When he'd taken her hand in his, she'd felt a security she'd never imagined possible with a man...especially a white man. She'd gone so far as to suggest he return for her to check his wound. Had he no idea how vulnerable that suggestion made her? Had he not glimpsed the hope in her eyes?

Apparently not, for while a couple of soldiers had ridden by in the last few days, none of them had been the commanding figure she secretly yearned to see. Had he taken care of the wound as she'd instructed? Men were apt to skip details vital for recovery. The cut could still have become inflamed, the blow to his head could have caused complications. And she would have no way of knowing.

How disturbing that she was even fretting over this.

While Ned turned the wheel to open the gate and the waterwheel began its *thump-thump-thump* rotation, Anna scraped a big pile of dirt out the open front door—and stopped on the stoop. Riding into the yard was the very man she'd been ruminating on, followed by two other mounted soldiers. Her heartbeat stuttered. But why did he have men with him? And the expression on his face...there was no spark of recognition. No cheery wave or joyful greeting. Indeed, his countenance reflected all business, as though she were a stranger.

"Miss Walker." He spoke as he swung down from the brown stallion he'd so carefully cradled her on during their return from the stickball match. He stepped closer, seeking her gaze. "We are here upon report of a firearm having been discharged on your premises."

"A firearm?" She stepped back into the doorframe while Ned came to stand behind her. "You are here not to check on our safety, but to accuse us of wrongdoing?" Her heart pounded now for an entirely different reason—one not nearly so pleasant.

"By order of General Wool, Cherokees are not to possess firearms. I'm afraid we'll have to conduct a search of your property." As the men behind him dismounted, Gage lowered his head the tiniest fraction, his eyes narrowed, then rubbed his temple. Did that mean something?

Either way, Anna took advantage of his distraction. She slid the hand not holding her broom behind her skirt and flicked it in a slight shooing motion. A shadow shifted as Ned made for the back door. Agidoda was helping Crow haul cane from Long Swamp Creek this morning, but her nephew knew where her father kept the musket beneath the floorboards. Could he get to the cabin without the soldiers detecting him?

She attempted to stall them. "Who made this complaint, if I may ask? Isaiah Thompson?" Her lip curled over the name. And she didn't have to work hard to infuse her tone with ire. That Gage would follow military orders so stoically clarified which side he was on.

"A neighbor of his—and yours. Malcolm O'Kinney." He gestured for his men to tie all three horses to the hitching post. Was she wrong, or did his reply sound more terse than normal?

Anna blew out a breath. "Malcolm O'Kinney will say anything Isaiah Thompson tells him to. He rides under him in the Pony Club. When does he say this happened?" A quick glance revealed that Ned had taken advantage of the soldiers' backs being turned to dart from a stand of trees into the house. He would take the gun to Crow's cabin.

"The day your mill was broken into." Gage shifted his weight as he watched the two privates looping the reins.

"You mean the day you were wounded?" The accusation in her voice ought to remind him he'd defended her then. Declared himself their ally. Yet today, not an ounce of warmth emanated from him.

Still, despite herself, her gaze went to his upper arm. He

wore a new coat in a navy color that looked official, and he moved with his usual languid grace. But his head...was there a bruise lingering under his hatband?

"That's right." If he noticed her interest in his well-being, he gave no sign, but rather, he straightened suddenly and instructed the men who had turned to face them. "Start with the mill."

The two soldiers brushed past Anna to search inside.

Gage drew closer and lowered his voice. "You understand, it's not going to go well for me if I don't return with a firearm."

Her pulse raced as she stared up into his face, his tight jaw sporting a slight nick from his morning shave. His normally jewel-toned green eyes seemed dull, shadowed. He was directing her to give up her father's musket? "Did you tell them someone fired a gun here?"

"Of course not." Impatience edged his reply. "I was unconscious, if you recall."

"Of course I recall. It seems you are the changeable one, pledging your support and then leading men here to invade our privacy and take away our rights." She held the broom in front of her with both hands tight-knuckled on the handle, forward-facing and stiff as a sentry.

He let out a little huff. "Anna—"

"Sergeant, can you help me open this crate?" One of the men appeared around the side of the milling platform.

Gage gave a brusque nod. "Be right there." Once the private moved away, Gage leaned closer and spoke low and tersely. "*Give me something.*"

Her eyes flew to his. The jolt of connection between them brought instant awareness. She could trust him. But how could she satisfy his commanders and at the same time help keep her family safe? With the recent trouble at the mill, she couldn't surrender Agidoda's musket.

~

A few days after his search at Walker Mill, Gage tugged his hat down against the cool evening drizzle as he rode Colby back to Fort Buffington from Canton. The same two privates he'd commanded that day, Donald McCleary and Luke Ellerby, accompanied him while Private Wood rumbled along behind them in the wagon, whistling "Zip Coon."

Gage's presentation of Joshua Walker's .56-caliber pistol to First Lieutenant Warren Clayton must have satisfied the officer, for this morning, he'd given Gage the assignment of investigating some old firearms that had been found in the back of a storeroom in town. Though they'd selected a few muskets and rifles the troops could possibly use and loaded them into the wagon, the weapons had been in nowhere near as good a shape as Joshua's 1805 matched-set flintlock had been—a personal gift to him from the grateful light dragoon officer whose life he'd saved at Horseshoe Bend. It had pained Gage to accept the weapon from Anna, but her story that her father had fired it to ward off an intruder had been believable enough to allow the Walkers to keep the newer and arguably more effective musket...for now. The pistol would've been easier to hide. He planned to reassure them when next he saw them that the weapon would be returned once their family reached Oklahoma.

A lump solidified in his throat to match the one that still lingered on his temple. Reality pushed in. Come spring, chances were good that Anna and her family would be herded into the fort his comrades would build at the site of their current camp and then be shipped west. Such inhumane treatment turned his stomach. Could he stand by and let that happen? Yet what could he do? The laws of the land were against them...

Except for the exemptions expected for Cherokee women

wedded to white men. But the tension and mistrust in Anna's slight frame from the minute he announced his intention to search the mill, the tears in her eyes as she surrendered the pistol, had reestablished the harsh divide between them. And how could it not? Even though he'd done his best to protect her by ensuring men patrolled the area and then insisting he lead the search party so he could provide enough warning for her to come up with a plan, there was no way that could make up for the stark truth. He was the invader, she the invaded.

He'd needed to play a role the day they'd searched the mill and her cabin, but he'd done himself no favors with her by allowing his migraine to make his terse manner so convincing. He'd had three of the head-pounding, eye-aching, nausea-provoking headaches since Thompson knocked him out. The day of the search, he'd barely been able to ride, but he wasn't going to let that stop him from overseeing the assignment. All he needed was one more thing to ensure his failure as a soldier...and more importantly, failure to protect Anna Walker.

As they approached the inn owned by her friend, Mrs. Campbell, he couldn't help but wonder if the ladies would attend the service at the Hickory Log mission this coming Sunday. Brother Sweetwater had visited the military camp yesterday to invite the men to hear Reverend Evan Jones on his circuit through North Georgia. The urge to explain himself to Anna niggled in Gage's chest, but he pushed it away. Best he kept his distance. She didn't want him. Why *would* she choose him above her own family?

"Help!" The feminine cry drew his head up. A woman in blue came running from around the backside of the inn, arms waving. Mrs. Campbell!—though today, he might not have recognized her as the same polished lady he'd met at church, with the muddied hem of her work dress flapping and dark-blond hair trailing from her bun. "Please, help!"

Gage clicked to Colby and trotted the stallion over to her. "What's amiss, ma'am?"

With a hand on her chest, Mrs. Campbell heaved in a huge breath. "My son...my nephew...and a friend—they pinned down some men in my hunting cabin." She pointed past the inn, toward a swath of trees on the eastern edge of her property.

"What men? What did they do?"

"White men. Members of the Pony Club. They turned my hogs out on my cornfield. You've got to stop my boys before harm is done!" Her fearful trembling became a full-out shudder accompanied by a cry as a gunshot broke the evening hush, sending several swallows shooting up from the nearby garden with a hooting and flapping of wings.

Gage turned Colby toward the sound and included McCleary and Ellerby with the wide sweep of his arm. Together they thundered across the field and entered the section of russet oaks, sparsely yellow-flagged poplars, and barren smaller trees split by the narrow lane that turned off Alabama Road. Gage's pulse pounded through his head in tandem to Colby's hooves. After a few minutes of riding, they rounded a bend flanked by steep red banks with exposed roots and rocks—and almost plowed over a young man running toward them.

"Whoa!" Gage pulled back hard on Colby's reins. They narrowly skirted the newcomer, who threw his hands up— apparently unarmed. The boy, his thin chest heaving with labored breaths, must be around sixteen.

"Are you from Buffington?" he gasped out.

"Yes. Are you Mrs. Campbell's son?"

The fellow's tawny hair combined with his light-bronze skin made Gage anticipate the young man's nod. "Fisher Campbell. My cousin sent me for help. We caught the men who drew our land in the lottery turning out our hogs on the cornfield. They want to clear it to plant wheat. We drove them into the cabin.

We just wanted to hold them until you could get here." A musket popped from farther into the forest, and with a jerk, he looked that direction.

Gage frowned. "By firing on them?"

"They fired on us first."

So both parties *were* armed. This could get ugly.

Was it just him, or was the glare of the evening light intensifying?

Donald McCleary's saddle squeaked as the big man shifted his weight. "Cherokees ar'na supposed to have guns." His faint brogue only intensified his brusque manner.

"Only Uchilla has a musket—my mother's. She didn't know he took it." Fisher's brow furrowed as he appealed to Gage. "Please...I was coming to get you. You can't let them destroy our property."

Gage pressed his lips together. "How many are there?"

"Two of them against Uchilla and Smoke Sanders."

Smoke. Gage wasn't likely to forget that name. Why wasn't he surprised that Foekiller was part of this standoff? He jerked his chin toward Luke. "Ellerby, you stay with Fisher and the horses. McCleary and I will go in on foot." The younger man would be more patient with Mrs. Campbell's boy, while the Scotsman would prove handier in a fight. They'd originally been trained and armed for infantry, not mounted combat. They had their best chance of accurate firing on foot, should it come to that. He'd do all he could to ensure it didn't.

They dismounted, and with loaded muskets, powder, and cartridge boxes at the ready, he and McCleary set off down the lane. The drizzle helped mask their footsteps among the fallen leaves. A minute later, they crested a small rise. About a hundred yards downhill, the lane opened into a clearing next to a creek branch. Up ahead to the right, a figure in buckskin and linen hunched this side of a fallen tree, reloading a musket.

Gage gestured for McCleary to join him behind a boulder.

"Georgia Militia!" Gage broadcasted his voice to the square, squat log cabin. The tip of a musket poking through the barely cracked shutter testified that the occupants were indeed armed. An arrow stuck to the front door told him muskets weren't the only threat. Who had done what here? The first thing was to disarm both sides. Then they could ask questions. "Come out and surrender your weapons!"

The man downhill, who had startled when Gage announced their presence, left his musket on the tree and rose into a crouch as if to run.

"Dinna do it." McCleary's dry command grated across the distance between them, and the Cherokee—Uchilla, judging by his close-cropped hair—turned to face them. Avoiding making himself a target of the cabin's occupants, he knelt but lifted his hands into the air.

Gage scrambled down the hill while McCleary covered him. He snatched Mrs. Campbell's musket and shot a glare at the wide-eyed young man. "Where is your friend?"

Uchilla nodded to an oak tree that loomed on the edge of the clearing, across the road. A lithe figure squatted in a lower branch, facing the cabin, a bow in his grasp and a quiver full of arrows on his back. "He won't come down until the men inside give up their guns."

Fair enough. Gage motioned Uchilla back toward McCleary, then raised his voice again. "You there, inside the cabin—open the door and kick your weapons onto the porch."

A moment later, the portal cracked open. Two muskets slid out, one after the other. A voice called, "We don't want no trouble with the militia, but it's not us you oughta be pointin' those guns at."

"Slide the muskets all the way to the edge of the porch." Gage kept his gaze trained on the cabin door. There were several ways this could go bad. Why had he left Ellerby with the Campbell boy? Fisher hadn't been a threat. Every one of these men were. He was no more prepared for military service than he had been in Florida. In fact, less...because something was pricking tiny black holes in his vision with the tenacity Unisi had tenderized beef.

Not again. Not now.

A long leg emerged from the door of the hunting cabin, the boot toeing the weapons toward the steps. The same wheedling voice continued. "Those crazy braves attacked us, held us hostage. See that arrow on the door? They woulda shot us if we come out."

"*I'm* telling you to come out now, hands raised."

The speaker emerged as instructed—a tall, thin, pointy-jawed young man in a long brown coat with equally long stringy brown hair—but defiance hardened his features. "Think you're the massah of the plantation, don't ya? Mounted militia bossin' around locals same way you do Indians. Well, you're on *our* land. And we take care of our own business."

"That's right." A second man appeared in the doorway, his lanky height and shoulder-length blond hair unmistakable even with the black spots mushrooming before Gage's eyes—and his hands held only waist high. "Like my cousin said...my lottery ticket stub says this is my land."

Micah Thompson had drawn the Campbells' land? Of all the tragic ironies. "Even if that's true, it's not yours until spring."

"Well, I'm tired of waitin'. These Injuns need a little shove sometimes."

"That what your uncle tried to do at Walker Mill?"

Micah stiffened and peered into the forest, searching for him. "I don't know nothin' about that."

Could his penchant for Anna mean he'd truly been ignorant of Isaiah's actions? Even so... "You and your kin are in enough trouble. Be smart and kick the guns off the porch." Gage's finger tightened on the trigger of his own musket. He blinked hard and squinted at the cabin. What if the men didn't comply? Was he ready for a shootout? Was McCleary?

A rustle of leaves behind him alerted him to the private's approach. The sound distracted him only for a second—but it was long enough for Micah to lunge for his musket. Gage aimed for the man's arm and pulled the trigger.

CHAPTER 9

"*Were you trying to kill him, Sergeant?*"

Lieutenant Warren Clayton's accusation rang in Gage's head the next morning as he followed the row between ecru canvas tents that led to the officers' quarters. At least he could see clearly today. He'd been too sick last night to do much more than fall onto his cot. But his stomach twisted with an altogether different type of nausea as he answered Lieutenant Clayton's summons. Had Micah Thompson died during the night? Had Gage indeed killed a man?

The blacksmith's anvil clanging against metal at the forge competed with the hammering of construction at the mess hall. The two buildings were the only ones erected so far. Amazing, how slowly things moved in the army. Outside the kitchen, a couple of soldiers unloaded a delivery of foodstuffs and other necessities with crates stamped *candles* and *soap*. Gage bypassed them on his way to Lieutenant Clayton's tent. His knock on the main post produced a crisp command.

"Enter."

He did so, removed his hat, and saluted the man not much

older than himself seated at his field desk. "Sergeant Edmonds reporting as ordered, sir."

Lieutenant Clayton put down his quill and surveyed him. "You appear improved this morning, Sergeant."

"Yes, sir." The next-in-command to Captain Buffington had asked surprisingly few questions yesterday, dismissing Gage rather abruptly after he and the privates gave their report. His main concern had been getting Micah Thompson to a doctor in Canton. "May I inquire as to the health of Mr. Thompson?"

The lieutenant gestured to the only other seat in the tent, a wooden folding chair. Gage hesitated, then took it as the officer responded. "He'll recover. But you're lucky, Edmonds. A couple of inches in, and you would've hit his heart. And then we'd have an all-out war with the Pony Club on our hands. You want to tell me what you were thinking?"

Gage swallowed hard. Admitting his infirmity could cost him his military service, but better his health be in question than his judgment. He lowered his gaze to his hat, resting upon his knee. "I was aiming for his arm, Lieutenant."

"Are you joking? You're a better shot than any man under you."

It was true—target practice was an area Gage excelled at. His father had seen to that from the time Gage could hold a musket. "No, sir. Truth is, I haven't been right since that blow to my head at the mill. I've had several headaches. Bad ones."

Lieutenant Clayton sat back in his upholstered chair. "Why didn't you say something?"

Gage drummed his fingers on his hat. "I thought they'd get better, not worse. Yesterday, half my vision went." Shame flooded him. What kind of a weakling almost killed a man because he had a headache?

The officer gaped at him a moment before he swiveled back to his desk. "This afternoon, you'll go to the same doctor we sent Thompson to." He reached for a pass and his quill, then began to fill in the date and Gage's name. Before signing his own to the bottom, he cut a glance over his shoulder. "Whatever he says, I have to take you off active duty...at least for a while."

Gage stiffened. How could he keep an eye on Anna and her family if he was consigned to desk work or organizing supplies? "But sir—"

Lieutenant Clayton waved his hand. "No arguments. My response to this altercation between the Indians and the Pony Club will be under close surveillance. Whatever the reason, a local nearly being killed by a member of the mounted militia will escalate the tension in the area. We're both going to need to take a low profile for the time being. You understand?"

Gage offered a brief nod.

"It would go over better if I released you from service effective immediately. You only have another month before you have the option to muster out, anyway."

"Sir, please, don't do that." Gage had to complete his term of service if he was to fulfill his father's last request of him, even if he wasn't here to see it. And now he had a more immediate reason—one who looked equally fetching in men's trousers as she did in flowered calico. The late-December mustering-out date had begun to loom overhead like the piston of a stamp mill. He couldn't participate in the spring roundup any more than he could leave Anna and her family at the mercy of the military that remained. *God, what am I to do?*

"Thankfully, I have an alternative in mind." Lieutenant Clayton's words came as if in direct answer to Gage's prayer. He handed Gage the pass. "You learned Cherokee from your grandmother, did you not? Your...er...*step*-grandmother."

"That is correct."

"It just so happens, I have need of an interpreter. As you know, many of the Indians we encounter have no English. Headquarters at Fort Cass has approved Captain Buffington's request to hire someone from among the soldiers to ensure these conversations go accurately." The lieutenant eyed him. "Are you up to the task?"

"Yes, sir." *Thank You, God.* Gage could hardly staunch his relief. In such a role, he had a chance of promoting peace. And perhaps lingering to watch over Anna Walker, whether she would welcome his protective presence or not.

~

On the Saturday about a week after Gage and his soldiers searched the mill, Anna sat by the evening fire shucking corn while sweet potatoes roasted in the coals. As they often did of late, her thoughts swung like a pendulum between Gage Edmonds and her father's rejection. Rejection was what it felt like no matter what other names he called it— protection, preservation, peace. How could being left behind to marry a man she barely knew bring about those things?

And yet she couldn't get that man out of her mind. When he'd last come to the mill, he'd displayed none of the charm from his first visit. He'd seemed like a stranger, aloof and focused on his task, yet she couldn't shake the sense that something was wrong. He hadn't looked well.

A thump from outside the cabin stilled Anna's shucking. Was Agidoda back from slaughtering the hog with Crow already? She hopped up with the dried ear still in hand, crossed the room, and peeked outside. No one was in sight. A gourd container lay sideways on the porch. Must have been the wind. She shut the door and returned to her task and her thoughts of Gage.

Despite his abrupt manner and the reason for his last visit, he'd made clear his desire to help her. To spare her as much as he could.

Why would he do that?

Anna's fingers stilled, and she stared into the flames as she contemplated the potential reasons for that. Reasons that left her numb with disbelief. Originally, she'd chalked his interest in her up to his mistaken idea that she was fully white. Then later, a dedication to his duty in his Cherokee grandmother's memory, and perhaps to please a father with a distinguished military record. But this latest intervention went beyond duty. Conflicted with it, in fact. And that could only mean...

The door banged open, startling Anna, and Agidoda entered. The late-November breeze swirled a few dried leaves over the threshold and licked Anna's stockinged ankles. "Brr. Getting brisk out there," he said.

Anna popped up, setting the husking aside to slide her iron spider over the flames. She scooped a dollop of lard onto the pan, then crossed to the sideboard for the chunks of venison she'd diced earlier. Ned had been delighted to bring down a small doe that morning.

Her father bolted the door behind him. "Did you have a visitor today?"

Anna faced him from the sideboard. "No. Why?"

"There were some boot prints around the cabin. I must have not noticed them this morning." He shrugged as if to dismiss any concern, though the frown lines on his forehead remained deeper than normal as he turned from hanging up his hat and overcoat on a peg beside the door. "But perhaps Ned should stay with you when I am away."

"You're only a short walk up the path." Having the restless boy underfoot all day would steal the peace she enjoyed while completing her early-winter tasks now that the time she was needed at the mill was less. She crossed to the hearth without looking at her father. The comfort she'd always enjoyed in his presence had evaporated since the day she and Gage came upon the saboteur. "You must be hungry. I'll have supper ready in a few minutes."

"No hurry, daughter. I will smoke and rest." He came near her as she added the meat to the hot spider with a sizzle and took down his pipe and tobacco pouch from the mantel.

"How did the slaughtering go?"

"All finished. Our family will not want for meat this winter."

"Mm." Anna moved a chunk of venison before it stuck to the pan. Sudden tears filled her eyes. This would be the last fall slaughter. The last winter she spent in the cozy cabin with Agidoda. In the spring, everything would change. She almost gasped from the sudden pain and fear of it.

Oblivious to her distress, her father sprinkled his special blend of tobacco into the bowl of his pipe, then tamped it in. "Crow told me Micah Thompson got shot in a standoff at Mrs. Campbell's with her son and nephew...and Smoke Sanders. Also some militia, including Sergeant Edmonds."

"What?" Her heart dropping, she whirled from the hearth to gape at him. "Is he all right?"

One corner of Agidoda's mouth twitched. "Which 'he' would you be asking about, daughter?"

Heat that had little to do with the fire swept her face. She scrambled to cover her lapse. "All...all of them."

"Micah will recover. The others are unharmed."

"Who shot Micah?"

"Sergeant Edmonds, though he did so because Micah was reaching for his own gun." Agidoda's solemn tone answered the deeper concern behind her question. This would mean more trouble between the factions. And they were connected to all three.

"Tell me what happened." Anna removed the nicely seared venison from the flames. As her father related how the Cherokee boys had caught Micah and his cousin letting their hogs out to ruin Mrs. Campbell's cornfield, then attempted to hold them in the hunting cabin while Fisher Campbell went for the militia, she transferred the meat to a tin plate. "What will happen to them?"

Agidoda had lit his pipe and taken his customary seat in the rocker. The fragrance of his smoking brought a sense of peace along with another stab of nostalgia. "They were held under guard at Buffington a couple of days for questioning. Since the musket Fisher used belonged to his white mother, and he did not shoot anyone, they were let go with strong warnings. Smoke's bow and arrows were taken."

He'd be fit to be tied. And looking for recompense. But more importantly... "What about Sergeant Edmonds? If he shot Micah out of self-defense..."

Her father lifted his one shoulder. "I assume he is still at Buffington."

"You *assume*? Why wouldn't he be?" Her heart squeezed as if someone had tightened a wire snare around it. "Could he have...left? Been sent away?" Wasn't he just doing his duty? Yet it was no secret that most members of the militia favored the white settlers.

"Would you care if he had?" Agidoda's sharp gaze always saw too much.

"Father, please..."

That she called him by his English title seemed to bring him to a decision. When she started to turn away, he sat forward. Gestured to her upholstered chair. "Sit, daughter. I must speak with you."

"The meat will get cold." And she did not wish to have this conversation again.

"Cover it." He waved his hand to the sideboard.

She went to fetch another plate with the center indented and set it over the venison, then reluctantly took her seat. She folded her hands in her apron. "Yes, Edoda?" Resignation leeched into her voice like salt in the smokehouse floor.

Her father's eyes swept her with concern as he lowered his

pipe to his knee. "There are things I have avoided telling you, but now I fear my silence is driving you away. I see how unsettled you are of late."

"What things?" Now it was her stomach under assault. Something in Agidoda's expression made her lose all appetite.

"The truth of your heritage. You are Cherokee by adoption, by the way you were raised, but your blood is white."

By adoption? What did he mean? Anna shook her head. "Why do you say so? I know you are a half blood, and my mother English, but if I was raised Cherokee, isn't that worth more?" She had fought this battle against the matrilineal beliefs of her father's people—that a child's identity was defined by the mother—for so long that she was exhausted. She'd thought at least her father understood. "I belong with you. To suggest otherwise is...is hurtful." She looked away.

"Your blood is white." When she only stared at Agidoda after his strange repetition, he propped his pipe against the oil lamp on the table and sat forward, capturing one of her hands from her lap in his strong, callused one. His dark eyes bored into hers. "Hear me. You are my daughter. I chose you. That makes you more my child than anything else. And yet, now is the time for truth. The time for you to take your place among your people."

"What are you saying?" Anna struggled to anchor herself. A whirlpool of dread opened beneath her, threatening to suck her under. She fought the urge to jump up and run, but Agidoda's intense stare demanded she hear him out. There would be no fleeing this conversation, now or later.

He sat back with a sigh. "The story of how I courted your mother was all true as I told it...only, there was more. She had a wealthy white suitor favored by her father. When I met her in Tennessee before the war, your grandfather had no intention of considering me as a son-in-law."

Anna nodded. That came as no surprise. Captain Andrew

Meade had still been a formidable figure even when she'd attended the school he paid for near his home years later...until the students rejected her once they learned of her Cherokee father. She supplied the next chapter in her parents' love story, one she'd heard many times. "But then you distinguished yourself at Horseshoe Bend. You saved that dragoon officer. And when you came back to ask for Mother's hand, Grandfather consented to your union."

"He did consent." Agidoda splayed his hands on his knees. "But not because of what I did at Horseshoe Bend. Because your mother was already carrying you."

"No." The word ripped out of Anna like the breathless hoot of the owl that perched near the cabin of a night. He couldn't mean...

Her father sat forward with a creak of the rocker. "It was not her fault. There was no shame upon your mother. She was still just as pure to me as if...as if her white suitor had never forced her."

Anna gasped. "*Forced* her?"

He nodded. "I was a convenient answer to the dilemma your grandfather found himself in, as she had tried to run away rather than marry the *i-na-dv*." The snake. "It took her months of tender care to recover. But she did. We loved each other. And I loved you as my own."

"No, Father." Somehow, Anna stood on her shaky legs. "No, Edoda. I will not believe it."

He rose beside her and attempted to steady her by the elbows, though she shook him off. "Whether you believe it or not, it is the truth. I tell it to you now because it gives you the power to choose. Cherokee women have that right. So should you."

"But I'm not Cherokee!" The admission rasped out of her like a jigsaw over rough wood. The truth was too painful to put into words, but she must do it, in order for it to sink in. She was the illegitimate daughter of a disgraced socialite...and a rapist. "I am a nobody. *Tlagiloi.*"

"Anna, aqua danvdo, that is a lie from the serpent of old." Agidoda held out his hands, entreating.

But he wasn't Agidoda. She had no father. Her breath came fast as the awful fact settled into her spirit. "No wonder I've never belonged."

"You love this place. You belong here...with the sergeant." His voice, his eyes, pled with her. "As a white woman, your options are greater. I can send for papers that prove you and not the lottery winner are the rightful owner of the property. You will be accepted, but you need a husband when I am gone. He can help you secure your home—all we have worked for. Can you not see this?"

That he was trying even now to pawn her off was more than she could bear. A cry broke from her throat, and she fled the cabin before the man who had raised her to be what she was not could witness her tears.

CHAPTER 10

The polite but empty smile Anna gave Gage before Sunday's preaching decided him—he would speak with her after the service about his behavior during the search of the mill. He'd passed the ride to the Hickory Log mission with McCleary and Ellerby weighing the wisdom of staying away from her against his unnaturally strong desire to explain. Thankfully, the two privates had been too engaged in their own debate over the best watering hole in Canton to pay him any heed. That they'd chosen to attend a preaching service probably said more about their newfound loyalty to Gage after the good report of their service he'd passed on to Lieutenant Clayton than any hunger for God. But at least they were here now, sitting shoulder to shoulder with him in the packed schoolhouse.

They weren't the only soldiers present as December came a'calling, rattling the closed shutters and hurling dry leaves to the ground outside. Other militiamen mingled with the Cherokees in the crowd drawn by the middle-aged Reverend Evan Jones and his assistant missionary, Jesse Bushyhead, who translated the sermon into Cherokee. All listened with rapt attention as Rev. Jones read aloud from his sermon text, John 15:16–19.

"'Ye have not chosen me, but I have chosen you, and ordained you, that ye should go and bring forth fruit, and that your fruit should remain: that whatsoever ye shall ask of the Father in my name, he may give it to you. These things I command you, that ye love one another. If the world hate you, ye know that it hated me before it hated you. If ye were of the world, the world would love his own: but because ye are not of the world, but I have chosen you out of the world, therefore the world hateth you.'"

No doubt, the verses resonated with those present, most of whom were accustomed in one way or another to being despised by those around them. Rev. Jones called them to evangelism, to peace and love, eloquently, his eyes piercing through his square-framed wire spectacles.

But Gage's mind kept going back to Anna's smile. Had it been disappointment or resignation that haunted it?

Regardless, it was obvious Anna had given up on him. He could bear a complete snubbing better than polite distance. Anger would have indicated she still cared.

Yes, he had to make her see that he'd acted with her best interests at heart, although human frailty had kept him from doing so in the gallant way he'd wish to.

As soon as the closing hymn ended, Gage settled his hat back on his head and made a beeline for the door. McCleary elbowed Ellerby, and the privates exchanged grins at their sergeant's rapid retreat. No doubt, they'd realized the object of his attention was the same attractive young lady from their visit to the mill.

He found her just outside, bundled in a wool cloak, her be-flowered bonnet nodding as she spoke to the preacher, her gloved hand in his. She turned as Gage descended the bottom step, and the gaze she swept his way held him captive. Was that moisture sparkling in her eyes? Or was she pleased to see him? Either way, the words he wanted to speak fairly leaped off his lips as he reached her side.

"Miss Walker...I was hoping to find you here." He didn't think before extending his hand to capture hers. He bowed his head and brushed a kiss over her cotton-covered knuckles. She blinked wide at him, hastening the explanation for his eagerness. "How are you? Any more trouble at the mill?"

"I'm relieved to say there has not been. Perhaps the frequent patrols of the militia have helped."

He squeezed her dainty fingers. "I couldn't come myself, but I ensured your settlement was a top priority for the patrols."

"You did?" Her lashes fluttered as she drew her hand away. "Thank you."

"I also wanted to apologize."

Her eyes widened.

"Your father's pistol...I know it has sentimental value. I can't tell you how much I despised taking it, but it did seem to satisfy my lieutenant. I wanted to let you know..." He lowered his voice. "I will see that it's returned." He couldn't say the rest—that the gesture would have to wait until after their relocation.

"I will tell him. Thank you again." Anna's attention strayed from him, breaking the eye contact that made awareness jangle through him, as Mrs. Campbell came to her side.

Gage bowed to the middle-aged lady, whose green velvet muff matched the plaid of her light-wool dress. "Ma'am."

She tipped her head. "I don't know what Anna is thanking you for, but I wish to add my gratitude, Sergeant Edmonds. Your intervention and testimony on behalf of my boys likely saved them from standing before a judge."

The unaccustomed praise caused warmth to creep up from his collar and kept him from looking at Anna. "I call it as I see it, Mrs. Campbell."

"We need more men who do. Too many in authority are

blinded by greed and prejudice. I rest easier knowing you're patrolling our county."

He shifted his weight. "I appreciate your confidence in me, ma'am, but the truth is, I'm off active duty for the time being. Maybe forever."

A small gasp escaped Anna. "Are you in trouble for what happened last week?"

A low chuckle rumbled from Gage's chest as he rubbed his clean-shaven jaw, his gaze still averted. "Some of the officers were none too pleased I almost started a war with the Pony Club, but that's not the only reason." He met her eyes. "Seems the blow to my head at the mill has caused some difficulties."

Anna straightened. "What type of difficulties?"

"Headaches. Vision problems. The day I came to conduct the search...well, I was afflicted that morning, which made me a bit short-tempered, for which I do apologize."

"There is no need." When her small hand rested on his arm, he startled. The compassion softening her face furthered his amazement. "And I take it, the day of the shooting...?"

He nodded, unable to speak for a moment past the knot he attempted to swallow down. Then he managed to say, "Otherwise, I would have made the shot I intended—to Micah Thompson's arm."

"Of course you would have." Her flash of humor, hinting that she picked up on his accurate marksmanship being a badge of honor, relieved his discomfort.

Gage managed a brief smile before he sobered again. "But should you need me...either of you ladies..." He broadened his gaze to include Mrs. Campbell. "You have but to call for me at Buffington, and I will come in a moment. I'll be acting as interpreter for the army."

"Interpreter?" Anna's fingers tightened on his sleeve before they fell away—an instant loss. "That seems an excellent role for you, Sergeant."

Gage. Call me Gage. But again, he couldn't speak. She was pleased he was staying?

"And these headaches...have you sought treatment for them?"

The concern in her voice filled Gage's chest with warmth. "I saw the physician in Canton yesterday. He confirmed that extra rest and less strenuous duty for a while should see me to rights."

"Then you must certainly heed his instruction." The steadiness with which her eyes held his underscored her words.

Mrs. Campbell's speculative gaze toggled between the two of them before she stepped forward, drawing Anna's arm through her own. "Forgive me, but we should head to the inn. The roast will dry out. I would invite you to join us, Sergeant... and your men." She glanced at McCleary and Ellerby, thumping down the steps behind Gage. "But Anna has promised me a quiet visit, just the two of us, to catch up."

"Yes. We have much to talk about." The smile Anna turned on her friend made Gage's heart lurch. Would she ever look at him with that level of trust and affection? That he craved that very thing startled him down to the square toes of his boots.

Gage lifted his hat from his head and offered a slight bow. "In that case, ladies, I bid you good day. But perhaps I might see you at the mill again soon, Miss Walker?" He hadn't intended to be so forward, but the question snuck out of him with the sly boldness of a fox in a henhouse.

Her slight form stiffened. "I thought you weren't riding patrols."

Gage settled his hat with increasing unease. "I'm not, but neither am I confined to quarters." Would she rebuff him once she realized he was asking to call on her for personal, rather than professional, reasons? Had he been mistaken in believing she'd softened toward him as they'd talked?

She hesitated a moment, blinking in what appeared to be

surprise. Or was it dismay, and she was trying to determine how to escape without hurting his feelings? Finally, she murmured a response without looking at him. "If you would like, Sergeant."

Gage bowed as she turned away with Mrs. Campbell, uncertainty churning in his chest. What was he to make of such a guarded response?

~

The sermon had buoyed Anna in ways she'd never expected. Two hours later, seated in Peggy Campbell's parlor with a full stomach and a full cup of tea, the warmth of it lingered as tangibly as the fire upon the nearby hearth. It had been as if Reverend Jones was speaking directly to her, Brother Bushyhead's Cherokee translation driving home every point like a tent peg into soft ground. Ground fallowed by how her father had sought her out the night before, drawn by the sound of her weeping in bed.

He had embraced her and told her he had been wrong to think she loved the mill so much that she would be better off remaining with the whites and mixed bloods who managed to avoid the removal. If she wanted, he would take the secret of her English paternity to his grave, and she could go west with them. That would do his heart good. She was his last reminder of his dear Mary. He only desired what was best for her, but he would leave the choice to her.

Agidoda's assurance that he loved her and wanted her with him had softened much of the sting of his earlier words, though erasing them from her memory would surely prove difficult if not impossible. And then she'd seen Gage, hurrying toward her with unmistakable eagerness on his handsome face, and her heart had softened like butter on a hot iron spider. His apology, his concern for her, had stacked on top of the preacher's command—God's command—to *go and bring forth fruit* which had reverberated in her head like a clarion call, making her question everything. Making her question if her destiny *could* lie here...with Gage.

If she had read this apparent interest correctly. His request to call on her had so discombobulated her that she'd hardly been able to form a response. Could he really wish to court her, believing her to be part Cherokee, or was his interest shallow... temporary? Many white men married Cherokee women, but Anna had never considered such an alliance—partly because of her distrust of them, but in truth, if she was honest, because she never thought one would pursue her.

Peggy settled in the armchair across from her, cradling her own cup of tea in her lap. Taking a measured sip, she studied Anna for a moment. "You've been quiet today...introspective. Did the sermon get you thinking?"

"Hmm." Anna straightened. Peggy was the one woman who had proven worthy of her trust, but speaking of the deepest matters of the heart, even with her dear friend, gave Anna pause. But who else? She yearned for someone to share her burden, to help guide her. Peggy was older, wiser, and a strong believer. "I've always thought I was a Christian. Mama read to me from the Good Book, then the missionaries did the same at school. I prayed and asked Jesus to save me before I was ten summers. I thought I had chosen God. It never occurred to me that He chose *me*." She batted back sudden tears.

Peggy offered a gentle smile. "And that has special meaning to you." She made it a statement, not a question, making clear she understood why it might.

Anna dipped her head in a little jerk of a nod. Blew on her tea to buy time to steady her voice. Still, when she spoke, it faltered. "I've never been...chosen..." Whether the concept related to God or Gage Edmonds, she struggled to fathom it.

"But he did choose you, Anna. It says in Ephesians that God

chose us to walk in good works which He laid out for us beforehand." At Peggy's words, the assurance swelling her tone, Anna lifted her chin. "Before we did anything to deserve His grace and mercy. That means He has a plan for you."

She sucked in a soft breath. "That is what Rev. Jones said today...that we are to go bear fruit."

"That's right. Even in the face of those who hate us, just as Christ was hated but fulfilled His mission."

Anna nibbled her lip and tapped her finger on her china cup. Finally, she blurted out the statement burning in her chest. "Agidoda thinks I should stay. Keep the mill and marry a white man." She wasn't ready to tell even Peggy about her ancestry. That revelation was too fresh and raw to voice so soon. She would keep it close to her heart for now. Besides, her dilemma stood independent of that fact.

Peggy's eyes widened. "Oh my." She sat unmoving for a long moment, her gaze fixed on the happily dancing flames. "I admit, I have often wondered if I would stay, if it were I who had some Cherokee blood, and not my George." As her soft statement faded, she snapped her eyes to Anna's. "*Any* white man?"

Clearly, the shrewd woman already knew the answer, but Anna fidgeted with her teacup. She smoothed a nest for it among the folds of her skirt. "Father has Sergeant Edmonds in mind."

"Aha. I thought there was something between you."

"No...no! There is nothing." Perhaps she protested a bit hastily. She amended her statement. "Except respect. And gratitude, naturally, as he has come to our aid more than once."

"Respect and gratitude which dictate a goodly amount of touching, as I noted this morning." Peggy's voice deepened—with teasing, not reproof. Anna relaxed a little at the twinkle in her friend's eyes. "And he seemed interested in seeing you again. You know, he would make a wonderful escort to the Christmas Eve dance." She tapped her lip in speculation.

For the past two years, Peggy had hosted the merry event that served as a bridge between the Cherokee and white communities. She bedecked the inn with all manner of greenery, illuminated it with bayberry candles and whale-oil lamps, spread her table with holiday delicacies, and hired local musicians to provide foot-stomping tunes. Anna had attended with her father and enjoyed many a quadrille and reel. But at the moment, she fixated on Peggy's earlier statement—that of Gage's interest in her. "But to what purpose?" Anna shook her head. "I won't be played for a fool."

Peggy's brow furrowed. "What makes you believe he would do such a thing? All his actions thus far have shown him to be a man of integrity. And I believe he's genuinely concerned about the welfare of our people."

"I do too." She breathed out the admission so softly, Peggy might not have heard it, but with it went a fair amount of fight. Anna's shoulders curved inward as she cradled her tea. Speaking these things aloud confirmed them. She trusted and admired Gage Edmonds. She was mightily attracted to him. But... "What should I do about it?" She couldn't disguise the plea in her expression as she looked up at her friend.

"That depends on how you feel about him." Peggy sighed. "After my first husband, I could never advise a marriage of convenience. That is why I wed for love the second time, regardless of what everyone said. Could you come to love the sergeant?"

The stirring in Anna's heart supplied the terrifying answer, but the instant flood of awareness mingled with anxiety stilled her tongue. Thankfully, her friend went on in seeming oblivion to Anna's paralyzed state.

"If you could love him, then you must consider carefully

which you want more—a life here with him, or one in Okla-homa with your family."

"With *all* of you." Anna went cold as she said it. Peggy would be leaving in the spring as well. Now the words gushed out of her. "I cannot see how a life here without the people I love could feel anything but empty. How could love for one man possibly make up for all of that?"

Peggy set aside her cup and leaned forward to take Anna's hand. "Once you are truly in love, my dear, and loved back with equal fervor, you will know the answer to that."

Anna's heart thundered even as Peggy squeezed her fingers in reassurance. She held on as though the older woman offered a ferry line across a flooded river. That type of love would make her far too vulnerable. How could she let a man in where she'd not allowed her dearest friends and family to tread? "I can't."

Peggy seemed to understand what she failed to speak. "You must, or you will forever wonder. And once that great divide separates you…"

The ache of emptiness in Anna's heart gave testimony to the accuracy of her friend's warning. "You would have me encourage him."

"What I could encourage is that, should he seek you out, you not turn him away. But there is one far more important than Sergeant Edmonds whom I believe is knocking upon your door—your heart's door, that is."

"Jesus?" Anna fairly whispered the name. That all-impor-tant name.

"I see the same softening in you when you speak of the Savior that I see upon mention of the sergeant." Peggy sat back, releasing Anna's hands but not her gaze. "Could it be the time has come to deal with both?"

Anna took a sip of lukewarm tea to buy herself a moment. A gentle drawing vibrated through her chest, like the plucking and resonating of a harp string. Finally, she said, "I sense He wants me to ask Him about my future. But I'm afraid to. I should weigh the facts and be able to decide the best course."

"Scripture tells us that God's thoughts and plans are higher than our own. He sees far more than we can—facts and even more important truths we cannot readily see. His will for us is always the best. Would you wish for anything less?"

"No..." She swallowed. "But how do I trust Him with my whole life?"

Peggy twisted her lips to one side before she answered. "I see a parallel here. I think you must give Him the chance to show Himself faithful. That is, if you are willing to let Him lead you."

Which was more terrifying...relying on God or a man? That both loomed with equal trepidation told Anna she'd been relying on herself. And yet she'd reached a crossroad from which she had no notion of where to go. Peggy trusted God, and the peace in her countenance, in her home, was unlike any Anna had ever experienced. And if God had truly chosen her, Anna, an illegitimate daughter rejected by both whites and Cherokees, then how could she not wish to belong to Him? "I am."

A smile broke across her friend's features. "Would you like me to pray with you, then?"

Anna set aside her tea. "I would."

And after she did this strange and scary thing, she would do another. She would allow Gage Edmonds to call on her...if her ambivalence hadn't already chased him away. But just as she would not yet tell Peggy the secret she'd learned about her heritage, neither would she tell Gage. He would have to show her that he'd choose her regardless.

id-December rain and snow finally ceased spitting in his face as Gage rode into the Buffington encampment. *Encampment* was all he could call it, even after two months. Tools and building supplies had proven as difficult to come by in the area as medical equipment and physicians, forcing the militia to import necessities from afar. And that translated into many more weeks spent in a tent city than anyone had anticipated.

Gage suppressed a shiver as he dismounted and turned Colby over to a private who acted as ostler. With unseasonable cold bearing down on them, the night promised little comfort for either man or beast. When had he last enjoyed a hot bath or waking without numb toes? At least he might partake of some warm vittles in the enclosed mess hall. But first, he needed to unload his saddlebags and musket in his tent.

He strode down the lane with as much haste as his stiff legs allowed and turned under his canvas fly, already divesting himself of accoutrements. A motion at the door of his tent arrested him—a woman standing from a folding stool.

"Mrs. Campbell!" Gage propped his gun against the rough-hewn worktable under the awning. What was she doing here? His heart stuttered. "Is everything all right?" With Anna? For… why else would Anna's friend be here?

"Oh yes." Her hasty reply, reassuring in tenor, emitted on a puff of frosty breath. "I paid a call on your commander to issue a special invitation for all the troops but preferred to see you in person. Captain Buffington assured me you were due back soon." Despite the muff encasing her hands and the fur-lined hood of her wool cloak that cradled her face, her cheeks and nose glowed pink in the twilight.

"How long ago was that?" Gage dumped his saddlebags on the table.

"Oh…" The matron gave a dismissive laugh. "Almost two hours ago."

Two hours? "Mrs. Campbell! Do allow me to escort you to the kitchen for a cup of coffee. We can warm up there."

"No…thank you. Too many men. My Fisher has been keeping an eye on me. See?" She tipped her head toward the tree line some fifty yards distant, where the young man in his floppy hat and bulky wool overcoat waited with two horses. "Anna and I were sorry you missed Brother Sweetwater's fine sermon yesterday."

They were? Gage cocked his head. Why the reference to Anna? Could it be possible she'd missed him in the two weeks since he'd last seen her at church? "So was I, although I was able to hear Reverend Jones and Brother Bushyhead again at Widow Ragsdale's. Business has kept me there for nigh on a week, and before that, in other parts of the county." As it turned out, Lieutenant Clayton had not overstated the need for an interpreter.

"So I heard." Mrs. Campbell pursed her still-full lips. "I have a feeling the Thompsons got their ideas about my cornfield from what happened at the widow's place."

Gage removed his no longer effective leather gloves and

rubbed his hands together in a futile attempt to generate heat. "The same thought struck me. Members of the Pony Club are in league together."

The claimant of Mrs. Ragsdale's property had turned his own hogs loose into her corn one night. He'd followed that offense by sowing wheat in the destroyed field. Rev. Jones was spearheading efforts to recompense her. If his appeal to the army proved as effective as that of James Proctor, a Hightower Cherokee whose fishing trap and son's gun had been stolen, the Cherokees were unlikely to achieve satisfaction. But it had heartened him to give them a voice—and a chance—in the negotiations.

Gage brought the conversation back around to the most pressing matter at hand. "Are you here because...did Anna..." Why did he sound so eager? He made an effort to level his voice. "Did she send a message?"

Mrs. Campbell stared him in the eye. "It is I who have the message."

"Yes, ma'am?"

"I came here ready to berate you for your inattentiveness, only to learn of your deployment. She doesn't know the reason. You mustn't lose any more ground."

"I'm sorry?" What exactly was she saying? Her staccato statements rather resembled military tactics.

"Call on her. She is proud. She will never reach out to you, but if you go to her..."

"I'm sorry." He'd just said that. He swallowed hard, hope battering like a logjam in his chest. "Do you mean she'd welcome my...courtship?" The word wedged in his dry throat. Ever since his last meeting with Anna, he'd conducted an ongoing debate with himself over what "if you like" meant. Unfortunately, he'd been unable to reach a verdict before his translating skills were called upon.

A smile such as one gave to a slow child who had just

comprehended something obvious to everyone else broke warmly over Mrs. Campbell's face. "Now you're listening." She pulled a small white card from her muff and handed it to him. "I'll even give you a reason to call on her."

Gage read the neatly printed block letters.

THE PLEASURE OF YOUR PRESENCE IS REQUESTED AT CAMPBELL INN FOR A CHRISTMAS EVE FROLIC AND BUFFET SUPPER, 7 P.M.

He raised his gaze to the matron's. "You think she would go with me? To this...frolic?"

Mrs. Campbell's smile broadened to a grin. "I strongly suggest you waste no time finding out." Her blond eyebrows snapped downward. "And do not allow a bit of waspishness to put you off. She must be convinced of your sincerity."

"Yes, ma'am." Anna would be waspish? Would she even hear him out?

Her friend didn't even wait for Gage to stop gaping at her before she whisked away with her head held high.

How did one frolic? Gage didn't recall his long-ago dance lessons. But did it matter, if Anna Walker consented to be on his arm? He was beginning to think he might earn the right to have her there...just maybe.

~

The town of Canton, which currently boasted around a hundred households, was as new to Cherokee County as the rough-and-tumble gold mining towns of Auraria and Dahlonega were to neighboring Lumpkin County. Thus far, Anna had managed to avoid it at all costs. Until today.

How had she agreed to attend Peggy's Christmas Eve Frolic with Gage Edmonds? And then allowed her friend to talk her into a shopping excursion to find a new dress? It seemed she could refuse neither one of them, especially Gage with his sincere apology and perfectly good explanation of why it had taken him so long to call on them again. In fact, as he'd detailed the cases he'd translated on behalf of the Cherokees in the area, pride had surged in her heart. He'd left her no reason to be standoffish, as she'd planned when she thought him fickle or disinterested.

When he had asked both Anna and her father if he might escort her to the dance, Agidoda, true to his promise to let her choose her own path, had refrained from giving his consent until Anna gave hers. But the glow in his eyes when she'd agreed to Gage's request showed his approval, reminding her how much he wanted to pass the mill to someone in their family, to leave a legacy here.

She stood on the boardwalk after Peggy's driver let them off near the courthouse, as exposed in her green calico and brown cloak as if she wore buckskin. Rumbling wagons shared the street with mounted militia, churning through mud softened by the recent snow. Miners from the nearby Franklin and Sixes operations jostled past on their way to the general stores or saloons with picks and packs strapped to their backs. Women in woolen outerwear stood talking on street corners with market baskets looped over their arms. Loose hogs and stray dogs jockeyed for space with children bent on escaping their mothers' clutches.

Despite its initial appearance as a gold rush boomtown, like a beauty bedraggled by the hardship of the frontier, Canton possessed a softer side—the side that intimidated Anna. She hadn't missed the gracious frame homes with flower gardens, groves of mulberry trees, and stables they had driven past—homes owned by families with sparkling-white names like Brooke, Grisham, Galt, and Donaldson.

It was said that Judge Joseph Donaldson had brought a

hundred thousand silkworms to Cherokee County. William Grisham, who owned around a dozen gold parcels, had founded Canton and First Baptist Church, served as postmaster, and was slated to become the clerk of the new mint in Dahlonega, which would start turning gold bullion into bars and coins sometime in the next few months. They had already shipped over fifteen thousand dollars' worth of equipment up the Savannah River to Augusta, from whence it had traveled the rutted roads to the mountains by wagon. Like Dahlonega, Canton had aspirations to become much more than a boomtown. It symbolized the explosion of expansion and industry taking over her beloved hills.

So did the name above the shop Peggy led her to. *Thompson.* Did Peggy not realize who owned this business? Anna had heard Micah's grandmother was the best seamstress in Canton. She'd just never had cause to visit her fine establishment. Like most Cherokees, she'd been taught to make her own clothes, and she'd gotten quite good at it.

"Look at that." Her friend pointed to a gown on a dress form in the multi-paned window. "It would be perfect."

Anna could hardly drag her eyes away from the sign above the door. When she did, she shook her head. The burgundy material shimmered in the midmorning sun like spilled claret. In addition to the silk-taffeta coming far too dear, the scooped neck and elbow-length, ridiculously puffed sleeves would expose an excess of skin. She might as well parade into the dance like a turkey with its tail feathers fanned. "I could never wear such a lavish gown."

"Nonsense. Your father gave me more than enough to cover an evening dress."

Peggy didn't lie. Agidoda had counted coins into her palm with the eagerness of a shopper on his last spending spree. Then again, he was. Anna's stomach tightened. No doubt, he figured if he could buy her future happiness, the cost of ten yards of silk-taffeta trussed up into a frivolous confection would prove a small price to pay.

She tried another tack. "People would laugh me out of there. No, this dress will do just fine." She smoothed her hand down her calico—its material a Christmas gift from last year.

Peggy's burst of exhaled breath stirred a curl from her forehead. "You are not attending my dance in your church dress. Not on the arm of Sergeant Edmonds. No. You need to outshine the lily-white Gainesville belles his family might throw at him."

The truth of her own lily-white ancestry that Anna choked back prevented her protest as Peggy opened the door and nearly shoved her inside. A tiny bell jangled above them. An elderly woman in a neat wool plaid dress looked up from a catalog open on a tall wooden counter. She wore her white hair upswept with fashionable curls dangling before each ear. Behind her, the bolts of fabric stacked long ways on the shelves framed her like a rainbow.

"Peggy..." Anna attempted to smile and speak without moving her mouth. "That is Moriah Thompson."

Peggy wiggled her gloved fingers at the proprietress, who stiffened in obvious recognition. Peggy's smile, by contrast to Anna's, remained as relaxed and natural as her posture. She barely even lowered her voice as she said, "I know exactly who it is—the best seamstress in Canton, and I won't take less for your gown."

"But your cornfield..."

"If Mrs. Thompson knew of it, which I doubt she did..." Peggy spoke more softly now. "If she tells anyone I patronized her dress shop, it will only show I am above such underhanded dealings. I go where I wish and do what I wish. In fact, I have even invited them to my dance, just to show there is no ill will."

She had? Admiration for her friend's refusal to be bound by the ties of class and race battled with unease. What if Mrs. Thompson also knew Anna had turned away her son and grandson at Walker Mill? She swallowed another protest. She did not share Peggy's imperviousness to social snubbing.

"Miss Walker."

Her name, spoken in such an inviting tone, drew her head up. Mrs. Thompson had slid off her stool and come out from behind her counter. She wore a generous smile. What was this?

"And Mrs. Campbell." Only a tiny twist of irony soured the name Micah's grandmother uttered without her pleasant expression faltering. "Welcome to my shop. How may I serve you today?"

When Anna failed to draw a breath, much less speak, her friend answered for her. "Miss Walker is in need of a dress to wear to my Christmas Eve Frolic."

"Oh? Is that so?" The scent of peppermint drifted on the breeze Mrs. Thompson brought with her. She swept Anna with a speculative gaze which Anna barely resisted cringing under. "You do realize, we're far too close to the date for a bespoke order."

"Yes, we are aware we will need to find something ready-made." Peggy's reticule swung from her wrist as she gestured to the dress in the window. "Naturally, this gorgeous creation caught our notice. If my eye does not deceive me, it might fit Miss Walker with the slightest of alterations."

"Oh no." Anna gave her head a rapid shake. "It's far too fancy. Perhaps we should look at what you have in the back." She glanced toward a rack of readymade dresses in serviceable calico and plain cotton. No doubt, Mrs. Thompson would agree such clothing was far better suited to her homespun lifestyle.

But the older lady clucked her tongue. "No, indeed, those will never do for a holiday party. Mrs. Campbell is correct. The dress in the window runs very close to your measurements." She started toward the garment in question, clearly expecting them to follow. "In fact, I made it in the hopes that a lovely young lady would want to wear it to a Christmas dance."

Lovely young lady? Anna managed to resist gaping as Peggy joined Mrs. Thompson in the window alcove, praising the fine tucking and stitching until Micah's grandmother giggled like a girl. What was happening here? The few times Anna had encountered the Thompson matriarch, the woman had gone out of her way to avoid acknowledging her.

Anna stood back until the ladies returned, the wine-colored gown now draped carefully over Mrs. Thompson's arm. The older lady held it out as if for her inspection. Anna trailed a cautious finger over a fold of the skirt, barely touching the butter-soft fabric. "I've never owned anything like it."

Mrs. Campbell tilted her head, her smile reflecting benevolence and the pride of one whose skill has been admired. "If you're worried about cost, I'm prepared to offer a nice discount. After all, as we mentioned, we're getting close to Christmas. I doubt there are any others who will come seeking such a gown —nor, I daresay, who would do it justice."

The woman was not only willing for Anna to try on such an expensive dress...she was so eager to make the sale that she was reducing the price? Something didn't add up. "I'm not sure it's practical." She darted a glance at Peggy, whose lips pursed in a mischievous smirk of a smile. No rescue there.

"Of course, it's not practical." Mrs. Thompson actually winked at her. "But every young lady should have such a dress at some point in her life. And my Micah has told me Mrs. Campbell's dance is the social event of the year. Why, I'm happy to say, he's recovered enough to attend, himself. And I'm certain it will do his spirits good to see you in this dress. So come along. The dressing room is in the back." She took off in said direction, upholding the dress with as much pomp as if it were the robe of a queen.

Wait...did Mrs. Thompson believe Anna might return her grandson's interest? She couldn't encourage such a notion. She sucked in a breath. "But I'm attending—"

The jab of Peggy's elbow in her side silenced her. Peggy tilted her head after the proprietress. Anna swallowed her protest and followed Mrs. Thompson to the dressing room, though everything in her advised caution. With the attention of two rivals fixed on her, such an evening threatened to bring about as much trouble as it did joy.

Gage couldn't wait to tell Anna his news—how he'd found a way to help her people that wouldn't compromise his morals. The offer Lieutenant Clayton had made him yesterday, the day before Christmas Eve and two days before the looming deadline of the end of his military service, couldn't have been timelier. No, couldn't have been more miraculous. The solution he'd tenured would allow Gage to stay near Anna during the days ahead, which would prove painful no matter which path she chose.

Yet the moment he saw her on the porch of her cabin had stolen all words from his head. She'd only allowed him a glimpse of her trim figure in the maroon silk dress before she covered it with a black cloak and gently pulled the hood up to rest on the gold filigree comb that graced her looped and braided hair. Her down-swept lashes as he complimented her hinted of shyness.

Shy? The miller's daughter who had stood up to Isaiah Thompson? While wearing men's clothing?

Indeed. Anna could hold her ground in the name of fairness and justice, but she clearly preferred to avoid the limelight in social situations. So Gage had done his best not to continue to gawk as he escorted her to the wagon filled with McCleary, Ellerby, and their local dates, who couldn't hold a candle to Anna's magnificence. Yet Anna didn't seem to notice, the way she greeted them and praised their appearances after Gage settled her beside him on the driver's seat.

He smiled and held out his elbow, offering to draw her close for warmth and security on the cold, bumpy ride to Campbell Inn. "You deserve to travel in a fine coach." He couldn't resist voicing the observation.

"Nonsense." She scooted nearer, her cloak protecting her skirt from the rough wood. "A wagon is all I've ever known." And to his delight, she slipped her gloved hand around his arm.

Gage could only hope his smile conveyed his pleasure. And the blanket he suddenly remembered to pull from beneath the seat and spread over her lap would convey his care.

Anna beamed at him. "Why, how thoughtful." Thankfully, she looped her arm back through his as he took up the reins.

With reluctance, he turned from the captivating sight of her and called to the team. He would wait until the end of the evening to share his news. If he could drop the other ladies off in the same order he'd picked them up, his men would allow him a moment to make clear his intentions to not only escort her to this one dance, but to court her properly. He'd already secured her father's blessing during a private visit to the mill.

"I've been meaning to ask you," she said as they turned onto the main road, "how are you faring with the headaches?"

He shot her a glance, brows raised. She'd been concerned for him? "Thank you for asking, Miss Anna." Perhaps she wouldn't notice the slight change of address. "They've been less frequent." No need to mention that exhaustion or bright light could still trigger them. So far, he'd been able to pace himself with the new set of duties.

"So they have not plagued you much with all this travel of late? Do tell me what you've been up to in the last week or so."

They'd been blessed with a frosty but clear night, the stars on full display. As they jostled along, he told her of the cases he'd helped with while she listened attentively.

"It seems you have found your calling, *Sergeant*." Her smile of approval, even accompanied by her teasing emphasis on his military title, meant more than the commendation of his lieutenant or captain. At least she was no longer calling him *Edwards*.

"I have, and it's one I plan to stick with as long as I'm needed. There's more I'd like to tell you about that later, but for now..." He dropped his voice so those in the back of the wagon wouldn't hear. Not that they were likely to, anyway, as they were somehow engaged in a rather raucous game that resembled pass the slipper, with Ellerby threatening to throw his lady's footwear into the bushes. Gage spoke into Anna's ear—or as near it as he could with her hood up. "Won't you call me Gage?"

"Why, Sergeant." She drew back in mock offense. At least, he hoped it was mock offense. Yes, a smirk danced about her lips. "I believe that is a familiarity reserved for courting couples."

He wasn't quite ready for this, but here was an opportunity not to be missed. His pulse raced. "Then perhaps you would consider—" Before he could finish, a small black object sailed over their shoulders and landed in Gage's lap.

Anna caught it before it could bounce onto the floorboards. "What's this?" She held up the heeled leather shoe, then swiveled to address the mixed-blood young lady she seemed to know well enough to be comfortable with. "Emily Snow, how are you going to dance the gallopade without this?"

"No better than if my foot freezes off." The girl shot a fuming glance at the guilty private. She held out her hand, and Anna returned her shoe, ending the game as well as the opportunity for Gage to declare his intentions. A few minutes later, murmurs and giggles from the wagon bed testified that harmony had been restored.

Lights blazed from every window of Campbell Inn as they approached, as well as from lanterns lining the drive. The tangy scents of woodsmoke and barbequed meat enhanced the cold air. As Gage pulled the horses to a stop, a servant appeared to take care of the team after the men helped the ladies from the wagon.

Bright notes of a fiddle and a piano beckoned them onto the wide porch, where couples seeking fresh air and men smoking pipes congregated. Once they crossed the threshold, the reason for the crowded porch became readily apparent, as they had to maneuver through the press of warm bodies into the foyer. Tongues of cold air from outdoors made the candles in the lighting fixture dangling from the ceiling flicker, casting shadows over the flushed and laughing faces below. Women whispered behind fans while men sipped strong drink. Older children sat along the banister decked with pine boughs. And here came Mrs. Campbell, pressing her way toward them like a steamship bearing upriver. Behind her trailed a handsome mixed-blood man in a black frock coat and pants and a white silk vest—the garb of a cultured white gentleman.

"At last, my dear." Their hostess drew close to kiss Anna's forehead as she put back her hood. "You'd better get into the dining room before there's nothing left." She leaned in again to speak in a stage whisper behind her hand. "I fear my invitation to the militia was well received, indeed. I have never seen so many *hungry* men."

Gage and McCleary and Ellerby responded with good-natured chuckles, and Gage paid their respects. "Thank you for having us, Mrs. Campbell."

"It's my pleasure. I'm just so glad you could come." The smile she spread between Gage and Anna filled in the blank of a missing word—*together*. After introducing her husband, George Hummingbird, she held out her hands. "Let me take your cloak. It will be on my bed when you're ready to leave. You simply must show off that glorious dress."

There was no denying the flush that spread over Anna's cheeks as her friend divested her of her wrap. It only deepened when Miss Snow and the other girl, whose name Gage had promptly forgotten, gasped and chorused their praise upon sight of her. There were other women in evening dresses— stuffy town matrons whose attire outshone their own beauty. Not so with Anna. She stood out like the poinsettias among the greenery. Did she not know it was not the dress but the way it enhanced her inner beauty that drew the admiring gazes?

If Gage had his way, she would never cringe under another person's assessment again. He quickly offered his arm. "Would you like some refreshments?"

The other four were already moving toward the long dining table groaning under the weight of barbeque, fried oysters, roasted nuts, candied fruit, tarts, and puddings. But Anna shook her head as she laced her fingers together through the crook of his elbow. Did Gage dare hope the prospect of spending the evening together robbed her of all appetite, as it did him?

Perhaps not, for she studiously avoided the stares of a trio of young women—pale-faced girls whose sour expressions and whispered exchanges revealed their resentment of being eclipsed by Anna. Gage made a point of catching their eyes and offering a small bow, sans smile—just to let them know their behavior did not become them.

Not noticing his silent censure of her critics, Anna looked around as though searching for a familiar face...and not finding one. When the musicians broke into a rousing tune, quickly accompanied by clapping and feet stomping, she brightened.

Gage gave her a small tug. "Shall we join them?" His heart

lightened as she nodded. He'd be the envy of every man present.

Joining the reel proved easier said than done, however, as the line of facing partners stretched from one end of the double parlors to the other. One ran the risk of sashaying into the unplastered wooden wall and sticking there. And then, the moment after Gage released Anna to take her place across from him, a skinny, unfamiliar youth from town—judging by his fine wool suit with its prominent gold watch chain looped across his waistcoat—stepped between them and asked Anna if she would like to dance. As though Gage wasn't standing right there...

While couples do-si-doed beside them, Anna's mouth opened. Clearly, she was so startled that Gage had to refrain from answering for her. "Thank you..." She had to speak up to be heard. "But this dance is already claimed."

The boy followed her wide-eyed glance to Gage, who narrowly resisted the urge to announce that more than the dance was claimed...and then remove the upstart. As it turned out, Gage's height and military bearing did the trick without him needing to utter any threats. Anna's would-be partner whisked from between them just before a galloping couple swept him down the aisle.

When Anna's gaze met Gage's, they both broke into laughter.

Thankfully, country dances could be performed without much recall of the instructions he'd received before he'd ever conceived of wanting to dance with a girl. But tonight...oh, he did. Taking Anna's gloved hands in his as he turned her about and stared into her dark eyes didn't bring her near enough or let him touch her long enough. Something had shifted since she agreed to spend her Christmas Eve with him. Did she feel it too? The energy, the connection that hummed between them? That need to be close?

When the reel tune turned to a waltz, he didn't care what etiquette said about dancing twice in a row with the lady you'd come with. He bowed and held out his left hand. Joy washed over him when Anna came to him as naturally as if they'd been dancing together all their lives, her steady gaze trusting. She fit so well in his arms. Before Gage could step out to turn her in the tight circle allowed by the limited space, someone tapped on his shoulder. Rather forcefully—which made his inclination to ignore the interruption impossible. As did Anna's raised brows and parted lips as she stared at whoever stood behind him. He knew who it was before he turned.

Micah Thompson. He wore his hair slicked back from forehead to collar, and a striped vest and black frock coat someone must have picked out for him, for he looked more respectable than Gage had ever seen him. Though the determination in his eyes said he'd trample boundaries to get what he wanted—which right now was Anna Walker. "I think it's time you let her dance with somebody else, Mr. Mountie."

Gage bristled more at the bumpkin's obvious omission than at the insult to himself. "I didn't hear you ask her."

Micah shifted his beady eyes to Anna. "Miss Walker, may I have this dance?"

"Thank you, Mr. Thompson, but I'm...I'm afraid..." Her gaze slid to the doorway, where a white-haired lady in a shiny plaid dress stood watching. Who was she? Anna swallowed visibly, then lifted her chin. "I've already promised this dance to Sergeant Edmonds."

Gage barely kept his jaw from dropping. One glance from Micah, and he clamped it shut.

The other man balled his hands into fists at his sides. "I see how it is. Well, don't worry. I won't be askin' again."

Some edge, some emphasis in the turn of phrase had Gage straightening to his full height. But Micah turned on his heel and stalked away. When he reached the older lady's side, she put her hand on his arm, and they exited the parlor together.

The music and dancers swirled around them for a moment until Gage and Anna both released their breaths. She gave him an apologetic smile. "Truly, I have no idea why he would do that. I've given him no reason to hope."

Gage shook his head. "Any man would be a fool to give up easily on you, Anna."

This time, she didn't correct him. She merely stepped into the frame of his arms, and slowly, carefully, he twirled around the inn's parlors. Gage managed to avoid treading on her hem or bumping them into any other couples...until a man with a glistening forehead whose vest lacked sufficient length to cover his ample girth bobbed his petite partner like a boat on a current directly in front of them. Gage shifted Anna into the open doorway just in time.

"So sorry." He grimaced in regret as he lowered their joined hands, his other hand still on her waist.

When two giggling girls, arm in arm, pushed into the parlor past Anna, he drew her closer. In what seemed a reflexive gesture, she leaned into him and rested her free hand on the lapel of his coat. He sucked in a quick break, and her gaze shot up to his, vulnerable. Startled. Then even more surprised as it raised just above him...where a cluster of mistletoe dangled.

Without pausing to think, Gage lowered his head—and encountered the cheek Anna turned his way. He lifted away with a twinge of disappointment. But it was quickly allayed by the smile that quirked up her lips and the twinkle in her eye as she peeked at him from under those dark lashes. And by the fact that she did not move, not even an inch. Her soft curves remained molded to his side as though God Himself had cloven her to fit there.

"Gage Edmonds, you persist in claiming liberties best reserved for a suitor."

A rumble of mirth vibrated through his chest. "At least you've changed *sergeant* for *Gage*, so I suppose I'm finally getting somewhere."

Her expression turned serious. "Where is it you wish to get?"

Oh, that he could tell her well enough, but better not to reveal the end goal he pictured, lest his ardor frighten her away. "To begin with, out of the army." He'd meant to wait, not to declare himself in a public place, but his growing desire to ensure no one else attempted to come between them made him almost reckless. He squeezed her a bit closer. "After tomorrow, I'll no longer be a soldier."

Instantly, Anna straightened, creating distance between them. "What do you mean?"

"My term of enlistment is up. Sixty-seven men, even our captain, will muster out. A bunch of new recruits have arrived, many from here in Cherokee County. They'll take the places of those of us who choose not to muster in again the same day."

"Including you?" Her face went pale against her gown's vivid hue.

"That's right." Gage attempted to recapture her hand but failed when she slid it behind her back. "But Anna, you should know—"

"I thought you said you wanted to stay to help. That you were happy being a translator."

"I am. And it allows me to be close to you."

"Which won't matter after tomorrow. Because you're leaving." Her chest heaved with a sudden breath. "I should have known." She turned abruptly and headed for the front door.

"Anna!" He reached for her, but the crowd closed around her. "I'm not leaving!" A sudden uproar drowned out his protest. Gage followed Anna through the press of bodies congregating around the door of the dining room, where the lights had been extinguished—all except for a blue glow that indicated a bowl of brandy had been set afire for a traditional game of Christmas Eve Snapdragon.

She made it to the door. And there was the lady in plaid, turning to her with an expression of exaggerated concern, touching her arm. Micah stood in the threshold just behind her. They both wore overcoats now as if prepared to leave. What were they saying to her? Why was Anna talking with them?

"Anna, wait!" Gage spoke loudly, but again, the merry-makers in the next room raised a hue as, no doubt, the first brave contestant had reached into the flames to snatch a burning raisin, or snapdragon, and popped it into their mouth. A group of rowdy soldiers hastened across the foyer in front of him, blocking his path. By the time they cleared, Anna and the Thompsons had disappeared.

He hurried outside as an enclosed carriage pulled away from the inn. Now he'd not only lost his opportunity to further his connection with Anna—she'd left with their mutual enemy.

CHAPTER 13

$\mathcal{A}$nna allowed Mrs. Thompson to cradle her arm as they bumped along in the enclosed coach. To warm her or support her? She'd tucked a blanket over Anna's lap, clucking over the fact that "the poor girl" had left without her cloak. After that, blessedly, the older woman refrained from speaking, providing Anna the time she needed to gather her composure. The darkened countryside offered only a few flashes of light to illuminate Micah's face opposite them. She shoved down her unease at being in such close quarters with him. His grandmother's presence provided safety and propriety—and soothed the flames of rejection ravaging Anna's heart.

How could she have imagined that Gage's invitation to the dance signaled anything other than an evening of diversion? An opportunity to steal a kiss from a pretty girl? Peggy had been wrong. Why would she suppose a man like him would tie himself to a mixed-blood county bumpkin and settle for running a gristmill when, with his background and education, he could have any city-bred lady he chose, and a career that would take him far from this rough-and-tumble frontier? He had no reason to love this land as she did. Or her.

Perhaps she shouldn't have fled in the manner she had. But tears had pressed all too close as that familiar feeling of rejection devoured her self-worth. She could not allow him to see her like that.

At length, Mrs. Thompson squeezed her arm. "I'm sorry the evening was a disappointment for you, Miss Walker, but glad you entrusted us to see you safely home."

Anna managed a response past her swollen throat. "Thank you."

"It doesn't surprise me. Soldiers are rarely the upstanding sort."

Micah growled from across the way. "If he did anything to dishonor you..."

"He did not." She spoke quickly. The last thing they needed was another confrontation. "I simply wanted to go home and would not request that he leave before his friends were ready." Her explanation fell flat when clearly, she had been escaping the dance when Mrs. Thompson stopped her to ask if everything was all right.

Micah's perusal felt palpable even in the semi-dark. "I knew he was making you uncomfortable—actin' like you were his to command. It's not enough he bosses around upstandin' settler men. Now he's got to take over our women too."

Anna bristled. "I am not...*taken over*."

"Well, that's a small mercy." Mrs. Thompson patted her arm. "You're with your people now. And you surely do look pretty in that dress."

Her people? What did that mean? Anna puzzled a moment before dismissing the first comment to focus on the latter. "If I do, it's thanks to you. It was your handiwork on display."

"No, my dear..." The older lady chuckled softly. "It's God's handiwork. I merely wrap it up pretty. Isn't that so, Micah?"

With a rustle of clothing, the figure across from them shifted. "Sure is."

"You know, my grandson has admired you for some time, Miss Walker." Mrs. Thompson leaned sideways to better view Anna. "In fact, he was planning to ask you to the dance if that arrogant sergeant hadn't interfered. But perhaps we can make up for that. Say, a dinner at my house in Canton? I lay quite a spread for New Year's."

Unease snaked around Anna's midsection and coiled, squeezing out a little breath. What had she gotten herself into? Forever reckless. "Thank you, Mrs. Thompson, but my family will need me. I'm the cook, you know."

"I'm sure they can make do without you for one evening."

"I don't know..." How could she graciously refuse this invitation? The ride home ought not to be made in stony silence.

Mrs. Thompson pounced on her hesitation. "My dear, you should broaden your horizons. Open your mind to new possibilities. With the right connections, you could play an important role in the future of this community."

Anna stared at her, trying to discern her expression in the darkness. Her tone and words...so benevolent. But... "I think you're overlooking an important factor, Mrs. Thompson."

"What is that?"

"In the spring, I will be leaving with my family." Especially now that Gage would be out of the picture. Her stomach clenched at the thought. Gone...as though he never existed. How had he burrowed into her mind and heart so quickly? This was why she kept her guard up.

Mrs. Thompson withdrew her hand from Anna's sleeve. "Surely, that is a choice you can make, not a foregone conclusion. With the proper support, my dear, you will secure a place here." Her firm reply tendered no doubt as to where that support would come from.

To be left behind with the likes of the Thompsons? Despite this woman's apparent kindness, her grandson had sought to foul Peggy's land, to force her from it. Anna's stomach twisted.

How could she have forgotten that? She'd been desperate and hurt, and she'd seized on the first opportunity to run from the man who'd broken her trust—that was how. But it was no reason to encourage these people now.

"I belong with my family." She spoke as firmly as Micah's grandmother had.

"You belong with your people." There was that term again. Disdain dripped from Mrs. Thompson's sharp statement, once more making clear her sentiments...and her understanding. But how did she know? How could she?

Anna's insides went hollow. Agidoda had sworn to tell no one the truth of her ancestry. Had he broken that promise? Never before had he betrayed her, lied to her. But how could it have been anything else? Suddenly, Mrs. Thompson's attentiveness in the dress shop and again tonight made sense. So did the attentions of the young men, *white* men...and the stares and whispers of the ladies, whispers she had thought had been about her striking attire.

"Stop the carriage." She had to get out of here. Now. She had been the worst kind of fool.

Mrs. Thompson's hand fluttered over her heart like a restless white moth. "But my dear, we are not to your home. Why, we must be half a mile away, at least!"

Enough of the show of civility. "I will walk the rest of the way." Anna knocked on the roof, but the upholstery absorbed the rapping of her knuckles.

"You will ruin your dress. Do not be ridiculous. Did *we* not come to *your* aid?"

"I am no longer in need of aid." Anna knocked harder, and the carriage began to slow.

"Think, Anna." Micah slid forward on his seat. "I could help you. Protect you."

"Help yourself, you mean." She gathered her skirt in one

hand. "And I didn't give you permission to call me by my given name."

His face hardened, so close to hers that his hot, sour breath fanned her cheek. "I'll have land of my own, remember. Together, we'd—"

"My friend's land!" When she reached for the door handle, his hand shot out and grasped her arm. "Let go of me." Panic choked her voice. She didn't wait for the driver to jump down and lower the steps. Instead, as soon as the carriage nearly came to a stop, she shoved the door open.

"Wait." Micah attempted to hook his arm about her waist, but she broke free and leaped to the ground. She landed with one foot angled to the side. Pain shot up her ankle, eliciting a strangled cry. "Anna?" He leaned from the carriage.

Her heart rate sped, and she grasped the yards of skirt fabric again and hobbled as fast as she could go with icy air nipping her exposed neck and forearms and tongues of fire licking up from the foot she'd twisted.

"Let her go." Mrs. Thompson's crisp command rang from the interior of the vehicle. "Foolish girl."

Yes. Foolish girl. Too mortified for relief, Anna kept walking as the jingle of the metal and squeak of wheels told her the driver was turning the carriage around, leaving her alone on the darkened lane. But somehow less frightened of the panthers and bears than she had been of the human predators who had pretended to befriend her.

Somehow, some way, she would figure out her own path, without relying on anyone else. Especially a man who would want her for what she could bring him, who would take everything she owned and leave her dependent and vulnerable, just as the white settlers had done to her people. For whatever her blood might say, her heart spoke louder. The Cherokees were the people of her heart.

For the third time in less than twelve hours, Gage stood on the Walkers' front porch and knocked at the door, Anna's weighty black cloak draped over one arm. Despite the late hour, he'd insisted on stopping last night after McCleary and Ellerby dropped their dates off. They'd waited impatiently in the wagon while Gage shifted from one foot to the other, his persistent rapping going unanswered even though voices could be heard from inside upon his approach. Voices that been strained, if not raised, in argument...which only intensified his need to speak with Anna.

So did the questions that now gnawed at him. What had happened since she left Mrs. Campbell's with the Thompsons? Had she been safe? He had to know the answer even if she never wanted to see him again. But surely, once he explained his plans, that would not be the case. He couldn't have imagined the affection in her eyes and touch before their misunderstanding. *Her* misunderstanding.

Indignation stirred. She hadn't even stopped to listen. Why was she so bent on finding a reason not to trust him?

Again, no answer. Gage stepped to the edge of the porch. Chickens clucked about, foraging among the frosty leaves at the edge of the barren brown woods. The mill wheel sat silent, the building's doors and windows shut with no sign of occupancy. Boot prints led away from the house, up the trail along the creek. Yet a plume of pungent smoke from the cabin's chimney confirmed someone was still home.

He faced the door and spoke as calmly and convincingly as possible. "Anna, I know you're in there. Don't you think you at least owe me the courtesy of hearing me out, after you ran off on me last night? Please..." Calm and convincing failed as unexpected emotion got snarled up in his voice like a rabbit in a snare. "I need to know you're all right."

A thump preceded uneven footsteps, and the front door swung open. Anna stood there in a nutmeg-brown woolen work dress, her eyes dull and puffy. Her long, dark braid hung down her back.

Alarm shot through him at her bedraggled appearance, and he stepped forward. "*Are* you all right?"

"I'm fine." She held the door against her as if prepared to close it on him at a moment's notice—with the same guardedness reflected in her face.

At a loss, Gage shoved the woolen garment he held forward. "You left without your cloak."

"Thank you." She accepted it, her other hand still on the door. "So now you may go."

Gage snatched off his hat and gaped at her. "Did you not hear me? Clearly, you didn't...any more than you did last night. I'm not leaving, Anna. I'm mustering out today, but I'll still work for the army...as an independent contractor. Lieutenant Clayton got permission to keep me on as a translator."

For a moment, something that resembled hope flickered over her face, bringing it back to life. Just as quickly, her expression shuttered. "That's good. I trust you will use your skills to help our people as much as you can until we leave." Again, she turned away, intending to shut him out, but he shot his hand forward and caught the door.

"*We?*" Gage pushed in behind her against the dictates of propriety, given the fact that they appeared to be alone. This time, he'd not let her dismiss him so easily, though he didn't have long before he had to return to Buffington. "Anna, doesn't this make any difference to you? It means I can stay. I can call on you..." His attention faltered as she crossed the floor in front of him. Why was she limping? "You're hurt. What happened last night?"

"Doesn't matter." Anna draped her cloak over the back of an

upholstered chair near the hearth. Placing her weight on one leg, she lowered herself into the seat. She extended one foot so that her moccasined toes peeked from beneath the hem of her skirt and reached for a pair of carding combs lying atop a basket of fluffy, speckled wool nearby. As Gage came to stand before her, hat in hand, she released a sigh. She didn't look at him as she spoke. "I suppose you've heard the same thing Micah did...that I'm white."

"What?" The world seemed to stop despite the motion of her carding combs. Their scratching sound failed to produce any friction in his brain.

"Yes." At last, her dark eyes met his, levelly and without emotion. Not a good sign. "About a month ago, Agidoda finally told me the truth. My mother was already expecting me when she married him. In fact, it was the reason she married him... through no fault of her own."

What was she saying? "Your father...was a white man?"

A single nod, and she diverted her attention to her carding, though she kept speaking. "Agidoda only told me because I was so hurt he wanted me to stay."

It was the thickness in her voice, the pause that followed the statement, which made Gage drop into the rocker facing her. He leaned forward, his hat on his knee, willing her to continue. To feel his support.

"You know I attended Tinswattie." Her gaze flicked up.

The local Baptist school at Hickory Log. Gage dipped his head, doing his best to conceal any confusion at the apparent change of topic.

"After that, my mother sent me to a small school being started near her family in Tennessee." Anna's face twisted, and she snatched out a snarl in the wool. "But their influence meant nothing once the girls there found out about Agidoda. You see, he had promised not to tell anyone the truth. To let them believe... But it didn't matter. My manners were too unpolished, even for my white family. When I tried to run away, they sent me back."

"That was their failing. Not yours."

She lifted her shoulder. "It was no better at Spring Place, where they shipped me next."

"Why was that?" Gage kept his tone gentle. Regardless of what might've prompted this sudden rush of honesty, whatever he did, he didn't want to shut down her sharing—not when she'd barely let him in the door.

"My mother was not Cherokee, which makes me not Cherokee in the eyes of the people."

How that must have hurt. The urge to enfold her in his arms swept over him so strongly, it took all his willpower to remain in his seat. Something in her manner warned him not to verbalize his sympathy, much less try to touch her. He nodded his understanding instead.

"So you see, I'm used to not fitting in. Not being chosen."

With a stabbing in his chest, Gage drew in a quick breath. "That's why you were so quick to think I was leaving. But I'm not. I was going to ask you last night if I could court you."

His revelation did not produce the hoped-for response. In fact, it produced little response at all. Only a question. "And did you know what Micah did...that I was white?"

His mouth fell open. "Did I...? No. I had no idea." Unease blossomed in his middle. "How did he find out?"

Anna sighed. "At first, I thought Agidoda told someone. But he assured me last night he did not. There was a time...we think someone was outside the cabin, though we don't know why."

Gage stiffened, his free hand drawing into a fist. "For no good reason, I'm sure. And something happened last night for you to hurt yourself." He glanced pointedly at her moccasin. "Did Micah harm you?"

A quick shake of her head set his pulse almost to rights. "I made a hasty exit from the carriage." She grimaced.

Gage could only imagine the reason for that, though doing so did nothing to assuage his temper. "He'll be angry. Angrier than before." All the more reason for him to stay close. His chest tightened as he shifted his gaze over the worn floorboards.

As if reading his mind, Anna tilted her head, her eyes narrowed. "Why have you been so set on protecting me? Even before you knew me."

Her skepticism showed she wasn't ready for the real answer, so he chose the standard one. "Isn't that what a gentleman, a soldier, does?" He made what he hoped was a casual gesture with one hand.

The carding combs went still. "I think it's more than that."

Perceptive woman. Could he put nothing past her? "If I can protect you, I should." He shifted. Looked away from her penetrating gaze. "I couldn't protect my sister. My twin."

"What happened?" She twisted some wool onto her finger.

"Some boy, much like Micah Thompson, wouldn't leave her alone, wouldn't take no for an answer. I tried to stick up for her, but at sixteen, I was scrawny, small for my age. He was older... and bigger. The mess he left me in convinced me, as well as my father, that I needed toughening up, and the military was the best place to do it."

"But you stood up for her. Surely, that was enough."

Gage laughed without humor. "Not for the Edmonds name, it wasn't. Especially when it did nothing to save her reputation. The scoundrel spread rumors about her, forcing her to marry an older man just to get away from the situation. Which is why..." He risked looking at her. Her eyes glimmered with life again. "Which is why I think women should have choices. And I'll support yours."

She sucked in a soft breath. "You truly didn't know I was white."

"I didn't. Anna, I don't care who your parents were. It's you I..." The truth stuck in his throat, surely too premature to be spoken, though she stared at him as if hanging on his next words. Before he could reassure her further, conviction rushed in. It was time he owned what he'd overheard on this very spot. "Though I did take in part of the conversation you had with your father and brother when I was wounded. As I was waking up. I knew your father wanted you to marry a white man, to secure the mill...and that you didn't want to."

"And yet you kept calling. Why did you do that?" She cocked her head to one side.

His heartbeat stuttered. "At first, I was trying to leave you alone. I wanted to respect your wishes. But then I saw you at church, and I thought...I thought you might feel the same about me as I did about you." He swallowed, waiting for a sign from her. The lack of one left him flustered, just when he'd sensed her softening. "And then Mrs. Campbell said you would be open to me calling. She gave me the invitation..." He trailed off as her countenance shifted from impassive to closed.

"It would seem not only my father but my best friend have interfered where they should not have."

"Was it so wrong that they encouraged me?"

"Yes." Anna stood, placing her wool in her chair. "For once, I wanted someone to want me enough to pursue me on their own."

"Even when you left him in uncertainty as to your own feelings?" Gage shot up inches in front of her. How dare she play with him this way, winding him around her finger like a skein of yarn? "Can no one ever satisfy you, Miss Walker? What will it take to convince you of my devotion? That I lay down my life for you?"

Her lips firmed as she stared at him. "That will not be

necessary. You may be staying, but I am going. The revelation my father made was good. It showed me who I am in my heart."

She would go with her Cherokee family to Oklahoma? The truth struck him with the force of a stamp mill. "You won't even give me a chance."

That could only mean her feelings didn't match his. But no, he didn't believe that. Desperation rose as she turned for the door, clearly intending to lead him out. Gage reached for her arm. Her unsteadiness worked to his advantage, and she stumbled into him. She turned her face up, eyes wide with surprise, lips parted.

This time, he was quicker than she was. He sealed her mouth with his. His fingers dug into her back, pulling her to him. After a moment of shocked stiffness, she made a little sound and caved, lips and body melding to his with a sudden fervor that confirmed his suspicions. Her feelings did indeed match his. In fact, they promised more ardor than he'd dared to dream.

Sweet exaltation had just begun to spiral up in him when she pushed him away. Anger sparked in her eyes. "You're just like the others, despite your fine words about women choosing." Her words came fast, her chest rising and falling with shallow breaths. "You take what is not yours. I have had enough of white man's ways. I will go west with my father and do my best to make a new life there. And you will go back to yours."

CHAPTER 14

A fiery sunset licked the western horizon as Anna and Ned closed up the mill on a Friday at the end of February. A hawk soared in the high-pressure sky, his sharp eye fixed, no doubt, on the darkening land below in search of prey. The air as they walked toward their cabins stirred with a surprisingly soft mildness, tinged with the hint of damp earth and pine. Though she welcomed the break from winter's harsh hold, the fair day had done little to lift Anna's spirits.

Almost two months had passed since she sent Gage away. Two whole months. Each day should have eased into numbness and resignation but only intensified the hollow ache in her chest, reminding her that something had been carved out of her and was missing. Sometimes, when she thought of him... far too often...her stomach even swirled with a nauseous sort of misery. Where was he? What was he doing?

Then there were the awful moments she glimpsed mounted militiamen, and her heart would leap. But every time, it was not him.

Peggy, whom Anna had avoided except for brief meetings at church, would advise her to seek Gage out, tell him she had been wrong. But that was just the problem. She wasn't wrong. They were from two different worlds, as evidenced by all that was happening around them. Even the die-hard optimists among the Cherokees were losing hope as Principal Chief Ross's efforts in Washington failed to bring the anticipated results. White settlers grew bolder, committing more flagrant depredations against the native people in an effort to drive them off before the deadline, impatient to sow spring seed on stolen land.

Word circulated that the Dahlonega mint had opened, despite a leaky roof, a water pump that didn't work, and a lack of copper and silver necessary to the coining process. The new superintendent had borrowed a thousand dollars and sent his assistant to Charleston seeking copper for the ingots and ordered staff to haul water from a nearby well to power the steam engine. The opening of the mint told the Cherokees how confident the government was that the white settlers were there to stay.

Not to mention the increased military presence evident on the roads and in town. When Anna and her father had ridden past Buffington for the last service before the Baptist missionaries had withdrawn from the region in discouragement, hammering had rung forth as officer quarters and stables were constructed. Wagons of supplies rumbled in and out. Agidoda had heard that Fort Buffington would become a supply depot for other posts, complete with a hospital ward and an armory. Two blockhouses would follow the erection of quarters for the men before the encampment was fortified...stockaded... prepared to hold in any Cherokees who had not departed before the May 1 deadline.

The place took on an aura of dread and threat. Anna avoided passing it whenever possible. And yet, her heart still yearned toward it, for the man she loved was there.

Oh no. No. It could not be. She stopped dead in the yard.

Ned nearly bumped into her. "Etlogi?" He tilted his scruffy, dark head as he studied her.

Her mouth went dry. She managed to shoo him toward the path. "I'm fine. You go on." With a nod, her nephew loped ahead. He must've grown an inch this winter. And how he loved helping her at the mill. It set him apart from his siblings. He would make an excellent miller. *Would have made.* Her chest constricted, and she called after him, "Ned?" When he turned, brows raised, she added, "Thank you for your help today."

He flicked his hand in her direction. "*Wa-na-hi-ge-s-do-di.*" Easy.

Yes, it had been a single order they'd opened the mill for—a Cherokee farmer with a big family who had emptied his corn-crib for meal. Still, it had felt good to do something useful, even for an hour or so. What would she do in Oklahoma? Just tend house for her father? Would they even have their own house, or would they be forced in with Crow's family or that of one of her other half siblings? How long would it be before they could save enough to purchase a mill? Would such a thing even be possible after they were reduced to nothing?

As soon as Ned rounded the bend, she pressed her hand to her burning chest. She couldn't be in love with the sergeant. They'd spent such limited time together. And yet, two months after not laying eyes on him, the draw to him remained just as strong. His words haunted her.

"I thought you might feel the same about me as I did about you."

She'd assumed he'd allowed pressure from her father and friend to push him into pursuing her for the same sort of motivations Micah Thompson possessed. Yet his words, his actions, said otherwise. How could she have lumped him in with a scoundrel like Micah? She'd been too het up with the injustice of her situation to see clearly. Had she made a terrible mistake?

While she stood there frozen with uncertainty, the cabin

door opened, and her father's sturdy form filled the threshold. He gestured to her. "Come in, Daughter."

She made her feet advance toward another night of mundane tasks. "Of course. You must be hungry." Her father and half brother had spent the day sowing oats in the far field. The rich scent of manure from the newly turned potato patch told her they'd been at work there as well. "It will not take long to heat the stew."

"The stew can wait." He held out his hand as she removed her cloak at the door. "We have company."

For a moment, her heart lurched. Had he come...finally?

Anna handed her father her wrap and cocked her head to peek around him. Not Gage.

Crow sat at one end of the table, his arms folded upon the board. Two strangers occupied the benches on either side, pewter tankards before them. No, not complete strangers, for she had seen them before—the day she and Gage stumbled upon the Cherokee youths carving the boulder by Walker Creek. Her pulse picking up, Anna stepped into the cabin. "What is this?"

Agidoda hung her cloak on a peg and gestured to the men, who had straightened and were gazing at her with interest, as though she was the person they had been waiting for. "Anna, I would like you to meet Yousannah and Arch Still from the Red Bank tribe."

Her gaze swung to her father, questioning, as she drew in a quick breath.

He gave a nod. "Our chief has put them in charge of mapping our land and hiding our valuables. They would like to speak with you."

Her hand went to her breast. "Me?" The customary unsettledness in her middle grew into a nervous fluttering.

Agidoda did not answer. The fire popped. The uncomfortable awareness was not just present within her—it hovered in the cabin like another presence.

"Please. Sit." Crow rose and held out his own chair, indicating she should take it before he retired to Agidoda's rocker by the hearth.

Slowly, Anna went forward and seated herself as her father did likewise at the opposite end of the table. Both young men offered somber nods as she looked between them. "What is this about?"

The one her father had indicated bore the name Yousannah wore his hair long and silver earrings in his stretched lobes in the style of some of the older men. He sat forward, extending his forearm on the table as he spoke in Cherokee. "I will trust that what I share will not leave this room."

She blinked rapidly and managed a nod.

"Two years ago, after the Treaty of New Echota was signed, about a dozen lower chiefs of Hightower met with our upper chief, Rising Fawn. Knowing our people would not be allowed to take our valuables to a new land, he invited our blood brother Jacob Scudder to be caretaker of our wealth, should the removal take place."

While Anna had grown up hearing much of Rising Fawn, a politician, farmer, and businessman who owned multiple properties including a gristmill on the Little River, and she was aware of the trust the local Cherokees to the east in the region called Hightower placed in Jacob Scudder, this was the first she had learned of such a meeting. A glance at her father's steady expression, however, confirmed that he possessed previous knowledge. How involved in this plan was he? Had these meetings been the ones that had kept him so busy the past couple of years? And why were these men laying out the details for her, when she'd already told Agidoda she intended to go west with them?

Yousannah continued his tale without reaction to any

unease she might have displayed. "They agreed to construct a tunnel to hide our gold, two hundred feet long with vaults for each depositor hidden by slab doors and an overhead deadfall to conceal the entrance. Each tribe would create sign trails to the tunnel using our ancient symbols on rocks and trees."

Anna shook her head. This sounded like one of the fables she'd heard throughout her childhood. "Are you telling me this tunnel is being built?"

The younger man, Arch, stirred on his bench. "As far as we know, it *has* been built."

"As far as you know? Are you not part of this?"

Arch glanced at Yousannah, deferring to him again. Yousannah sipped from his tankard before he answered. "Our chief was the only one who took exception to the plan. He does not trust the white sub-chief. Instead, he called a meeting of our tribe, and we agreed to hide our own gold."

Anna caught her father's eye. "And you gave permission for them to hide it here. On Walker Creek." His nod tangled her emotions into a knot. "Yet you know we are all leaving." As much as she tried to keep her voice even, it rose at the end of her sentence, revealing the hurt that once again surged in her heart.

Agidoda's expressionless countenance softened with regret and concern, and he leaned forward, as though he might have taken her hand if they sat close and it was just the two of them. "So I told them, but these men come at the request of our chief. We owe them the respect of hearing them out, at least."

Arch took that moment to lean down and heft something from the floor at his feet onto the table—a covered clay pot. From the *thunk* it made on the wood, it was quite heavy. "There will be two dozen of these. Families have already begun to bring their treasure for us to hide."

It was Anna's turn to sit forward. "You will bury them?"

"Along the banks and hillsides of the creek, yes, and in a smaller cave which we have concealed the opening to."

Curiosity stirred as she thumbed through memories of exploring the creek as a child. She recalled a couple of locations where a cleft into the rock could be expanded without too much trouble. She was about to ask when Arch lifted the lid from the pot, and she sucked in a quick breath. In the firelight, gold dust glimmered like sand ignited by a desert sunset. "All will be pots like this, full of gold dust?"

"Different sizes, different treasures, but yes, mainly gold dust. Our people have had many years to store it as we have worked the Sixes mine...since long before the white man came." Arch closed the pot and returned it to the floor.

"How will the people know where to find them if you are hiding them, and when would they return?"

"We are making maps that will lead them to the signs in the rocks and trees. Should you decide to safeguard this treasure the way Scudder watches over that of the Hightower people, we will give you copies of these maps. The people will return as soon as we feel it is safe, though it may not be in our generation. That is why we are taking such care...so their descendants can find the gold."

"But...you want me..." Anna couldn't get the rest of the question out. Her fingers picked at a fold in her skirt.

Yousannah's expression relaxed a bit, as if he understood the painful position they were putting her in. "We know it is much to ask. All along, your father has hoped you might marry a white man and hold onto the mill, this land. So he had told our chief. The chief put the plan into motion last year."

Anna cut a look at Agidoda. Had he also told them about her real father? The barest shake of his head relieved her fears of at least that much. She refocused on Yousannah as he went on.

"We have heard good things about the sergeant, Edmonds,

how he has helped our people and now gives them a voice as a translator. At your side, since you were raised as a daughter of our people, he is a man our chief would trust more than Scudder. We understand Edmonds has not come to visit in almost two cycles of the moon, and that it is your wish to leave with your family, but if this is something you would consider for your father's tribe, we would be in your debt."

With that, Yousannah bowed his head to her as though she was a Blessed Woman, a leader of their people. That gesture revealed the gravity behind their request. They, and more importantly, their chief, were entrusting her with a great honor. Regardless of her personal feelings, she must respond in kind.

Anna swallowed down her panic and returned the slight bow. "I will prayerfully consider." It was all she could promise at the moment.

Yousannah looked up with hope sparking his dark eyes. "For now, that is all we ask."

Another question pushed its way forward. "What will you do if I do not remain here?"

Yousannah's expression shuttered. "The land will go to the lottery winner. We stand a good risk the man will discover at least some of the gold before our people can return for it."

Arch reached for the clay pot, scooping it against his side as he rose. "Our people would express our thanks, of course, for the burden we place on you. Scudder will take one-tenth of the gold when the families return to claim it. We would expect you to do likewise."

One-tenth. A miller's toll. Somehow, that seemed fitting. It would also set her family for life. A family she might have... *might have had*...with Gage.

Her father saw the men out with a promise to have an answer for them in a fortnight. Crow bid them farewell and followed. As soon as their father had closed the door behind them and returned to her side, she met his gaze without attempting to conceal her anguish.

"Edoda, you want me to do this?"

He reached for both her hands. "I want you to do what your heart instructs you to."

"But I've told you...in my heart, I am Cherokee."

He lowered his head and fell silent for too long while her pulse pounded. Then he squeezed her hands and said, "In that case, what is the greatest service you can do your people?"

The heart they were discussing seemed to plummet to Anna's toes. "Even though I am white, I would need a husband to help run the mill and for safety, especially given this new responsibility. There would be danger."

"There would be danger, yes." The lines by Agidoda's eyes creased with his smile. "But I know a young man not only accustomed to danger but who seemed very interested in the job."

She groaned and pulled away. "That was before...before I ran him off. It's too late. I told him I did not trust white men and I would leave with my family."

"And yet, I have watched you drag about these past two months with a face as long as a bottle gourd and shoulders as droopy as those of the scarecrow I put in the garden."

She couldn't deny it, though she tried to hide behind her hand.

Her father pulled it away and spoke firmly enough that it compelled her to meet his eyes. "If he feels the same, it is not too late."

CHAPTER 15

The noise of a bustling fort reverberated in Gage's head at the end of the last week of February as he attempted to take down the statement of a Cherokee who lived along the Etowah. Each of the old man's emotion-choked words as he described how suspected Pony Club members had burned his barn deserved to be recorded in hopes of recompense and protection from the militia. He'd managed to get his horse out in time, but his prized milk cow had succumbed to the flames. The piteous mooing the man detailed churned Gage's stomach. All because some neighbors had apparently been offended when the Cherokee man had not pulled his wagon far enough off the road, into the muddy ditch, for them to pass the week before.

Still, it was hard to focus. Across Lieutenant Clayton's quarters, so newly built they smelt of fresh pine, John Wood was giving a report to the officer about the delivery being unloaded outside. Muskets, cartridge boxes and belts, bayonet scabbards and belts, flints, cartridges, kegs of powder, balls, and cartridge paper. Every item on the list Wood noted aloud intruded on

Gage's concentration. Instruments of war that made the report of one old Cherokee seem obsolete and pointless.

He blinked and rubbed his watery eyes. Sleep had eluded him the night before. The change in weather or perhaps something abloom in these parts seemed to have brought about a sore throat, cough, and runny nose. More concerning was the familiar throbbing at the base of his skull that foreboded a migraine. He hadn't experienced one in two or three weeks, and the bright light streaming in through the unshuttered window wasn't helping.

On his way to the exit, Private Wood stopped to stare at him. "You all right, Sergeant?"

Gage dropped his hand and straightened, attempting to look alert. "Not 'sergeant' anymore."

"Right. I keep forgetting." The younger man peered at him. "Say, you look rather flushed."

"I do?" Gage ran a couple fingers along his hairline, which came away damp. "Bit warm in here, is all." He unbuttoned his frock coat as he'd been longing to do for some time and shrugged out of it, draping it over the back of his chair while all three men stared at him.

Lieutenant Clayton's voice came from across the way, where his portable writing desk was set up next to a guttering fire. "Didn't you say some Indians in the village you visited last week had measles?"

Gage's stomach plummeted. He'd forgotten. "Yes."

Wood took a quick step backward. "You should go see the doctor."

A physician, Samuel Thompson, had been assigned to Fort Buffington as medical officer at the beginning of the month. Gage had spied him moving into a small empty cabin which would become the infirmary, though the lack of baggage accompanying him was concerning. Where were his books, his equipment?

"Can't." Lieutenant Clayton stood, approaching just far enough to get a better gander at Gage. "I ordered him to Fort Cass for supplies. Brought him in from afar with little more than his medical bag. He left a couple days ago. I can send for the doctor from Canton if need be, though I hear there's an outbreak of measles there too."

"No need. I'm sure it's just a headache." His scratchy throat belied his words.

The lieutenant cocked his head and narrowed his eyes. "Doesn't sound like just a headache."

Gage offered what aimed to be a casual grin. "Nothing a spring tonic shouldn't cure." Quill poised to write, he gestured for the Cherokee man to continue his testimony. Before he could do so, however, a coughing fit doubled Gage over.

Lieutenant Clayton spoke over Gage's futile attempts to catch his breath. "That's all for today." His words may not have been understood by the Cherokee, but his tone and gesture toward the door were. The man took a step in that direction, placing his floppy hat on his silver-shot black hair, then glanced back at Gage, his brow furrowed.

Gage managed to sit upright and offer a quick, reassuring smile. He spoke in Cherokee. "I have recorded your complaint. We will investigate and be in touch, I assure you." *Could* he assure that? If Gage was sick, who would ensure the native population received fair treatment? Not these soldiers preoccupied with establishing a fortress and armory intended to capture and remove them.

After the man left, Private Wood turned back near the open door. He lifted one eyebrow as he gazed at Gage. "You got spots in yer mouth?"

"I don't know." His patience was expiring faster than his ability to focus. "Wanna look?"

"Naw." Wood took another step back. "But my granny says

what can tell ye for sure is to get a quantity of sweet brandy and drink it down. It'll bring on the rash faster if it's measles."

"And why would I want to do that?" Gage signed his name to the document he'd just completed.

"I reckon if you'd like to get better quicker."

"I've heard the same. Not to mention the possible need to quarantine. So that sounds like the makings of a plan." Lieutenant Clayton adjusted the leather belt that cinched his dark wool frock coat in at the waist. He twisted his mouth to one side. "I'd just as soon both of you leave my quarters now. Private Wood, accompany Mr. Edmonds to the grocery just outside the fort. Make sure he drinks the brandy—"

"Sir, I don't drink." Besides, surely, a more traditional course of action would present itself.

Lieutenant Clayton frowned at the interruption. "Make sure he drinks the brandy and then, if the spots appear, you're to ride for the doctor in Canton while our translator sequesters himself in the new infirmary. We can't have an outbreak in camp. Or a panic about an outbreak, so say nothing to anyone else as of yet. Report back to me, Wood."

"Yes, sir." The younger man saluted, then moved onto the small porch to wait for Gage. He left a wide berth between them as they crossed the yard. Soldiers carried boxes and crates from waiting wagons into the two blockhouses of twenty-foot-square hewn logs with portholes that would allow those inside to fire obliquely, thus covering any potential approach of the enemy...the unfortunate people who had called this land home for decades.

Gage fought down nausea that had little to do with any illness. Was he fooling himself in thinking he was doing some good by staying here? The activity around him proved that the inevitable would occur. What could one man do to reverse it... or even delay it? Especially when the woman he'd most hoped to aid refused to see him.

Could he blame her? Not when his desperation to convince her of the connection between them had led him to treat her with less respect than Micah Thompson ever had. Gage's face flushed even hotter when he recalled the way he'd manhandled her. Expected her to melt in his arms as though he was the conquering hero. He didn't deserve her. Perhaps in Oklahoma Territory, she would meet a man who did. Perhaps she would finally belong somewhere. The fact that it was not with him squeezed the air from Gage's lungs.

Or maybe that was whatever ailment had hold of him. He'd never contracted measles as a youth, but he'd known of children who'd lost sight or hearing, whose seizures had led to mental disability, and who had lapsed into the grip of pneumonia and died. The disease posed an even greater threat to adults. The lieutenant was right to be concerned about a panic.

While Private Wood went into the little log grocery that an enterprising individual had thrown up about two hundred yards distant from the fort, Gage leaned against a nearby oak tree. A bird twittered overhead, heralding the approach of spring. But the barren limbs offered no protection from the winter sunlight as it pierced his closed eyelids with unnatural persistence. The trunk seemed to shift beneath his shoulder, and he startled back into an upright posture. He needed to lie down.

"Edmonds." Wood calling his last name from about halfway across the clearing sounded disrespectful after all the months of hearing his rank preceding it. Gage opened his eyes as the younger man placed a tall, corked brown bottle on a stump between them. "Here's your medicine."

Gage pushed off the tree. "You sure this will work?"

"Granny swears by it, and I don't question Granny." The assistant quartermaster moved away as Gage approached. He stood nearby, keeping a leery lookout in case an unsuspecting individual should draw too near.

Gage took up the bottle, uncorked it, and sat on the stump. He sniffed the contents. Sweet and strong, all right. "This might be the stupidest thing I've ever done."

Wood shrugged. "Lieutenant's orders."

Nausea assailed Gage as he gradually downed the alcohol, but he forced himself to finish it all. Sweat broke out on his forehead even as a hard chill shuddered through him, leaving his limbs weak and trembling. How could he even make it back to the fort? He lowered the bottle and wiped his mouth with the sleeve of his other arm. Thin linen. No wonder he was cold now. He'd left his coat in Lieutenant Clayton's quarters.

"Gage!" His first name called out in a feminine voice brought his hand down and head around. There, riding toward him on her mare, was Anna Walker. Her face beneath her bonnet lit with something akin to...hope?

Why did she have to be passing now, of all times?

"Anna." He staggered to his feet, and the bottle fell from his numb fingers. The busy street scene swam before him as the contents of his stomach hurtled toward his throat. Gage turned and stumbled into the enclosure of the fort. He managed to speak to the wide-eyed Private Wood as he staggered past him. "Keep her away."

He couldn't let Anna see him like this. More importantly, he couldn't expose her to whatever illness he was most certainly in the grips of. Even if it meant he never saw her again.

~

"I still believe you're jumping to conclusions." Peggy pulled the lid off the cast-iron pot hanging over the fire, stuck in a wooden spoon, and sampled the contents. "Mm-hm." Her sound of approval indicated completion, success.

The savory scent of chicken and dumplings filled her kitchen. She'd been in the herb garden when Anna had ridden by that afternoon. One look at Anna's face in response to her cheery wave, and the older woman had invited—no, insisted—that Anna come inside. And here she had been ever since, a lump of remorse and shame and hurt slumped over an untouched and now-cold cup of tea while her industrious friend bustled about preparing supper for her guests.

"What else is there to conclude?" Anna threw her hand up. "He literally ran away when he saw me. Or stumbled, more like. Which I could not make heads or tails of until I dismounted and went over and sniffed that brown bottle he'd tossed down. Drunk!" As if possessed of a life of its own, her other hand flew off her lap and knocked the honey twirler from a nearby saucer.

Peggy straightened and frowned at her. "I cannot imagine Sergeant Edmonds to be the type of man to retreat to a bottle... even if he *is* heartbroken over you."

Was that chiding in her tone? Anna's mouth dropped open. "I'm sorry, but what did I say to make you think that was the case?" She bent down for the honey twirler while her friend posted a hand on her hip.

"I saw the way he looked at you at my Christmas dance. Smitten. And then for you to turn him away as you did..."

"I didn't come here to be chastised."

"I know. You've been avoiding me for almost two months." The touch of heat in Peggy's tone hinted more at hurt than indignation, but the gentle rebuke still stung.

"I have not..." Anna's protest died away as her heart clenched with guilt. She could never be untruthful with her closest friend. "I have." Her lip wobbled, and tears sprang into her eyes. "But only because I'd begun to hope you might be right about Sergeant...Gage." She swallowed as the name left her throat raw. "And then it turned out like every other relationship in my life...except for the friendship with you. And today, when he couldn't even face me..."

"I understand." Peggy hurried over and touched Anna's shoulder. "Forgive me. But couldn't there be another explanation? What was it the private said to you after Sergeant Edmonds went into the fort?"

"*Mr.* Edmonds." Anna let her arms droop. "All he would say was that Gage couldn't see me now and that I should stay away from the fort. Which I would prefer to do, anyway. I wasn't even sure I could make myself go in there. Like a prisoner walking up to the gallows. I'd thought it such good fortune when I rode up to find him outside the walls."

Peggy shook her head. "Something is happening. Some emergency. I'm sure of it."

"But why couldn't Gage tell me so himself? Why run off and let another man speak for him?" Unless she had irrevocably severed any tie between them when she'd sent him away the last time, just as she feared. The truth was, she fully deserved every ounce of misery that coiled in her gut at this moment.

"Could he be in trouble?" Peggy lingered, meeting Anna's gaze, before shifting away to lower a stack of plates from the cupboard.

"I can't think what. As a translator, he is no longer part of the army. He's not under orders in the same way, even though he may have to fulfill his contract." She sighed. "I can only assume that same lack of military discipline might have led to him lowering his standards. Maybe the same sort of discouragement that many Cherokee men face now. He had so wanted to prove himself in this assignment. To make a difference. I never would have thought that of him before, but what else does the evidence suggest?"

Peggy took a few steps toward the dining room before pausing and turning back, the plates clutched before her. She shook her head. "I'm going to pay a call myself and get to the bottom of this."

"Oh, no, Peggy. Please don't."

The last time Peggy had put her oar in, it had only complicated matters. Anna would be better off if she'd never attended that dance with Gage Edmonds. If he'd never told her he had feelings for her and wrapped her in his arms for that bone-melting kiss. She'd tried so hard to be angry with him. Even allowed her words to lead him to believe that. But her ire had lasted about as long as dew on a sunny August morning. Longing and regret had quickly replaced it. The truth was, she'd already been contemplating how to undo her actions before her father challenged her to act on what was in her heart.

That hadn't meant going to the fort had been easy. Indeed, she'd arrived with no idea of what she would say, only a prayer and Gage's name on her lips. And the hope that one look in her eyes and he'd come to her. Instead, he'd run. The shame of it nearly crumpled her even now.

The tear that slid down Anna's cheek only seemed to solidify Peggy's resolve. "Yes, I will. I won't leave my friend hurting like this, especially when I am responsible for putting you in this position to begin with. There is a reasonable explanation, I am sure. If it's the last thing I do before leaving this land, I will see you and that man settled. One way or another. Besides..." She firmed her lips and her gaze intensified. "There's a lot more at stake than just your happiness, remember."

Anna straightened as Peggy resumed her course into the dining room. She drew in a steadying breath. She'd forgotten Yousannah and Arch had come not only at their chief's directive but at Peggy's suggestion. If anyone could bring about the desired result in this situation, it was Peggy Campbell. But did Anna want a man who so clearly did not want her?

No. And yet if Peggy was right and something was wrong at the fort...

"Make yourself useful and remove the bread from the oven,

will you?" Peggy's voice carried over the clinking of dishes from the next room.

That evening, after Peggy convinced Anna to stay long enough to partake of the hearty meal with her in the kitchen, she set out on her mare for home. The spring-like weather had tricked her into forgetting how early dusk fell this time of year. Small animals scampered for their burrows in the woods along the road, and a mourning dove called its soulful goodnight as a breeze rustled the leaves still clinging to the beech trees before new life pushed out the old.

The sun had bathed the western horizon in fiery shades that belied the chill of evening settling over the land by the time Anna reached home. No movement or sound from mill or cabin broke the stillness of oncoming night as she led her mare to the stable. She half expected to find Ned there, as he enjoyed tucking himself into a stack of hay to read of an evening during the off season. Indeed, he'd been there recently, for he'd left his book on the indented section of hay, but she unsaddled, brushed, fed, and watered her mount without the appearance of her young cousin.

A thin plume of smoke traced upward from the chimney as Anna approached the house, meaning Agidoda had probably heated the stew she'd left him for supper. She'd left the meal handy in case Gage had greeted her with open arms and they'd needed time to talk, to plan...

Regret pierced her sharp as an arrowhead. Had she really been so foolish? She needed to start thinking about what she would do if Peggy's reconnaissance mission produced only more disappointment.

Anna opened the cabin door and stood there blinking as she attempted to make sense of the scene before her. Items lay strewn about the floor, furniture overturned. Three men stared at her, obviously caught in the process of ransacking her home. Two of them, unfamiliar settler men in floppy hats and nondescript garb, one stocky and one tall and wiry, reached for weapons. Only one revealed any remorse...Micah Thompson.

Her stomach clenched. This was bad. Very bad.

And then a cry left her—for on the floor in front of Micah lay her father, a gash to his forehead seeping blood, his hands and feet tied. Unconscious...or dead. "Father!"

What did it say about her that she called him that instead of his Cherokee title? And what a crazy thing to think of in such a moment.

A gun clicked behind her head. Anna went dead still.

Isaiah Thompson came around from behind the door, a pistol trained on her and a wicked grin splitting his frayed brown beard. "Welcome home, Miss Anna. We've been waitin' for you."

CHAPTER 16

"Don't see no spots." Private Wood held the lantern he'd lit a bit higher and peered at Gage from the opening of his tent.

"Should they have appeared by now if they were going to?" Gage spoke from atop his cot, where he'd collapsed about an hour ago, shivering, boots still on.

The assistant quartermaster rasped a skinny hand over his lightly whiskered jaw. "Yeah. Should have."

Gage groped for his leather possibles bag on the small table next to him but only managed to spill the contents on the ground. "Hand me that mirror, would you?" He gestured to the object he needed.

Private Wood did so—actually, he tossed it onto Gage's belly—before stepping quickly back. He watched while Gage examined himself in the looking glass.

Behind the younger man, the sounds of the encampment setting down for the night carried on the brisk breeze that stirred the flaps of the canvas shelter. As a translator, Gage didn't merit a spot in the officers' quarters or even the newly constructed enlisted men's barracks. As inconvenient and uncomfortable as it was, his lack of a home only served to reflect his transitory status in life. Where did he belong? He'd wrestled with that question since coming to Cherokee County. He'd thought he'd found the answer, but…

Hm. Gage released the side of his cheek and frowned at his reflection. Wood was right. No spots—including no white specks inside his mouth, a telltale sign of measles. Relief flooded him. He clicked the mirror face down on the table, his arm falling back with unaccustomed weakness to the side of the cot.

A sudden realization hit with the force of lightning. Anna. She'd not been passing the fort by chance as he'd first thought. Had he been well enough to think straight, her expression, her tone, would have told him she'd come to see him. Gage pulled himself upright and swung his legs over the side, knuckles grasping the edges of his cot. His insides lurched, and the world swirled, but he managed to keep down whatever remained in his stomach. Which wasn't much. He'd deposited the majority of the rum into his slop bucket promptly after returning to his tent. Thanks to that, though, his head was relatively clear, even though a fever still sapped his strength.

"What are you doing?" Alarm raised Woods's voice an octave.

Gage almost chuckled. Just how convinced was the man of his grandmother's method of diagnosis? Didn't matter. "How did Anna react when you told her to stay away?"

"Uh…she didn't like it none, I can say that for sure. Got down from her horse as though she was prepared to argue her way in. Then she saw the bottle and went over and sniffed it."

"Oh no." Gage put his hand to his splitting head.

"Oh yeah." Woods shrugged, a grimace crossing his thin face. "I tried to explain, but quick as a trap springs, she hopped on her horse and galloped off."

Gage let out a low moan. "I've got to go after her." He

pushed himself off the cot and stood swaying a moment, hands fisted at his sides as he took shallow breaths. "Do me a favor and have the ostler saddle Colby?" He crossed to his small trunk where he could find an overcoat since his frock was still in Clayton's quarters.

"Bad idea. Measles or not, you're in no state to ride."

"Good point." He'd better take some backup. "I'll see if Ellerby and McCleary will come with me." Hopefully, the men still harbored sufficient loyalty to him to agree to ride out without the lieutenant's permission. Because the truth was, Anna would not have come seeking him if something hadn't been important enough to override her pride. And he'd just made matters worse by rejecting her when she needed him.

~

"Where is it?" Isaiah Thompson's sour breath fanned Anna's face, nearly gagging her.

"Where is what?"

"The map to the gold. I know you have it."

"I have no idea what you are talking about." She lifted her chin, but her voice wobbled. "Please. Let me go to my father. What have you done to him?"

The stocky, middle-aged man to Micah's right, who had been holding Anna's sewing basket, nudged Agidoda with the toe of his boot. "He's alive, if that's what ye're wonderin'."

A soft moan from her father confirmed the villain's words and wrenched Anna's heart. This was exactly what he had feared. They'd just never guessed it would come so soon.

"Though not for long, if you don't cooperate," Isaiah's voice growled in her ear. "Tell me what I wanna know, woman."

"Please..." Anna held her hands up. "I don't know what you mean. There's no map. I know nothing about any gold." Surely, a partial truth would be justified in this circumstance?

Isaiah hooked his arm around her waist as though she was a fish on a barb and snagged her to him before she could react. Anna stumbled into his side. The hard barrel of the pistol nuzzled with horrifying familiarity into the base of her skull. She didn't dare to breathe—though the stench of the man's unwashed body somehow invaded her nostrils regardless.

"We coulda done this the easy way. You coulda been part of the family, little lady. I'd a'welcomed that." His hot breath seared her neck, his lips so close they might have brushed her skin. Anna shuddered, and Micah took a step toward them. "Too late for niceties now. I don't cotton to impertinent females. I'm warnin' ya, young Micah over there won't be able to stop me from teachin' you a lesson if I run out of patience."

"I don't know what you think I know." Anna managed to force the words past her constricted throat, though they emerged almost in a whisper.

"A sight of a lot more'n I do, and I know enough. We saw them braves visit your cabin. We seen 'em creepin' around these woods. Bucks from all the different villages been doin' the same since fall, markin' the land, buryin' treasure. Our boys has got eyes and ears everywhere. And we know they make maps of where they hid the gold."

"Even if I had a map, you wouldn't be able to read it." A spark of defiance strengthened Anna's reply. "It would be written with the same ancient symbols that are carved on the rocks and trees, symbols only my people understand."

Isaiah seized her arm and spun her to face him. "Then you'd just have to translate it for me, wouldn't you?" He shook her hard enough that her teeth rattled together.

"Stop!" Micah's booted steps stomped across the floor behind her. "You promised you wouldn't hurt her."

"I said I wouldn't if she cooperated. But this one's sassier than a riled polecat. Don't know what you see in her." Despite his words, Isaiah released her, and she stumbled backward.

Micah braced her from behind, the clasp of his bony hands running a chill down her spine. Isaiah made a spitting sound, as if flicking something distasteful from his mouth. "She talks about *her* people. But she's betrayed her own. In my book, that makes her no better than the natives."

Anna blinked at him. "Betrayed my own?"

He glared at her. "We know what you are. We know about your pappy. Your *real* pappy."

Anna's limbs went weak. Micah had started to relax his hold on her but supported her by one arm when she faltered. She'd been right. And that explained Mrs. Thompson's attentiveness, as well as her grandson's and that of the other settlers at the dance. Still, she wouldn't give them the satisfaction of admitting the truth. To do so would feel like a betrayal of her Cherokee family.

Isaiah stepped closer, his pistol now pointed downward at his side. "And yet you'd chose these *people* over my nephew. Well, that was your mistake. Now you have two choices left. You can either lead us to the gold, or we'll burn this place down with you and your precious Cherokee father inside."

Anna sucked in a quavering breath. Could he mean it?

Micah stepped between them. "Uncle Isaiah, let me talk to her. Alone."

A crude laugh spilled from the older man's lips. "Bet I know what you really want to do to her...*alone*."

Anna cringed and lowered her lashes. Was she in danger of what he suggested? Micah had never been forceful with her, but all these months, his wheedling hadn't worked. What if his patience, too, had expired?

"Just a few minutes." Micah raised his hands. "That's all I ask."

Isaiah surveyed his nephew for a long moment before he huffed out a breath and stuffed his pistol into his belt. "Fine. But only a few minutes. And don't try anything you'll regret.

Lovesick whelp." Muttering the last under his breath, he motioned to the other two men, and they tramped toward the door. Isaiah turned back before pulling it closed behind him. "We'll be on the porch."

Anna wasted no time in running over to her father. She knelt beside him, her calico skirt pooling around her. "Edoda? Father, can you hear me?" She cradled his head. Slid her fingers around his throat in search of a pulse.

"He's still alive." Micah drew closer, coming to stand over them as, sure enough, Anna detected a thready pulse and slumped with relief. "I can't guarantee he'll stay that way if you don't do what my uncle says."

She lifted her face to him, frantic, entreating. "I don't have a map, Micah. I don't know where any gold is. Please, you have to convince him of that."

He shook his head. "He's like a hound on a scent once he gets set on a course. We know there's gold, Anna. You've got to come up with something, or I don't think I can stop him a second time from settin' fire to this place."

"A second time?" She came to her feet, her legs wobbly.

He pressed his thin lips together, and a hank of dark-blond hair nearly hid his profile as he turned his face from her. "The night I overheard you talkin' to him about your real pa." Micah jerked his pointy chin toward Agidoda, who still did not stir.

Anna let out a soft gasp. "The boot prints around the house. That was you?"

Micah gave a sharp nod. "Uncle Isaiah's wanted revenge since you wouldn't mill his corn last fall. He was set to take it that night. I convinced him to wait—that it would be better to own all this than destroy it. Since we learned you were white, he was willing to let me try."

"And then I turned you away after the Christmas dance." The noose was closing around her. She had no information to bargain with, and Micah would not help her. She needed to get her smelling salts from her herb box on the sideboard. If she could revive her father, together, they stood a chance of overpowering Micah, at least. Anna started in that direction, but he put out his hand and stepped in front of her. She blinked innocently at him. "I'm only going for something to revive my father."

"No, you don't. I'm no fool, Anna."

She lifted her chin. "My brothers will come." Only part of her hoped they would. The other part feared what would happen if they did. Crow would not hesitate to die defending them.

Micah's grim look almost conveyed pity. "We hid our horses well. By the time they get here, it will be too late. And remember..." He touched the pistol hanging at his hip. "We have guns. They don't."

Guns. Actually...

Anna barely prevented her gaze from sliding to the loose floorboard only a few inches from her father which concealed the musket Gage had left them. It was loaded. Could she pretend to be checking on her father and retrieve it quickly enough? Even if she did, could she actually shoot a man...shoot Micah?

Did she have a choice?

But she was not alone. *Please, God, help me.*

She let her shoulders and head droop as though defeated. With shuffling steps, she crossed back to her father's side and knelt there, taking his hand as though for reassurance. "Very well." She inhaled a quavering breath. "I will do as you say, though I spoke the truth in that I have no map. I will have to take you to where I believe the gold may be. But tomorrow, not tonight. We'll need daylight."

The corners of Micah's lips tipped up—if not exactly in a smile, in a gesture of satisfaction. "That's good, Anna. I might be able to convince my uncle of that. I'll go get him."

He turned toward the door. Here was her chance.

Anna lunged for the loose board. Rough wood snagged her fingers as they slid beneath the edge, and she tossed the board to the side with more haste than stealth. It thudded and slid across the floor.

Micah whirled. Worse, the front door banged open. Isaiah stood framed in the threshold, the flapping of his dark coat making him resemble an evil spirit from the netherworld.

Anna grabbed the stock of the musket and raised the barrel at the same time Isaiah drew his pistol.

Micah threw himself toward her.

A shot shattered the silence of the night. Or was it two, fired simultaneously?

A man's shriek carried from the doorway, but the crash of Micah's body into Anna's prevented her from seeing what had happened and loosened her grip on her father's musket. The weapon clattered from her hands. Micah grunted as his weight pinned her to the floor. In trying to shield her, had he taken a shot for her? Or had he meant to protect his uncle?

If the string of expletives from across the room was any indication, he'd failed.

Anna wriggled out from under Micah to glimpse Isaiah gripping his arm, his pistol on the floor. Bright red blood seeped between his fingers. "The she-wolf shot me! Get her." He jerked his chin from the other two men who had charged back into the cabin toward Anna.

As they leapt into motion, she struggled to her feet. Micah grasped her skirt, but she shook him off. She had to get out of here—run and get Crow. The gunshot would have alerted him. Maybe he was already on his way.

But behind her, her father stirred and moaned. How could she leave him?

The second she hesitated, glancing over her shoulder, gave

the stockier man opportunity to seize her arm. Micah tackled him around the legs. "No! She's mine."

"Get her!" Isaiah's crazed command rang through the cabin. "We'll burn this place down!"

"No!" Micah sprang up just as his uncle's tall comrade reached her. Micah's wild undercut somehow made perfect contact with the man's jaw, snapping his head back. As he stumbled, Micah looped an arm around Anna's waist as he drew his pistol. He swung it from one man to the other, covering their attempts to recover. "Back off." When Isaiah made an almost imperceptible move toward his own weapon before him on the floor, Micah jerked his pistol in his direction. "You too. No one touches this girl. I've waited too long for you to ruin this. No, everything will be mine yet."

"Have you lost your mind, boy?" Isaiah held up the hand below his wounded arm while staunching the flow of blood with the other. His face had paled, and the wheeze in his question made him less threatening. "What makes you think she's gonna want you now?"

"Because I can save all this." Micah tightened his arm around Anna's waist, squeezing as if to convince her...or claim her. "By tomorrow morning, she'll agree to marry me. Hold off that long on your revenge. That's all the time I need."

By tomorrow morning? Fear cinched her gut far tighter than Micah's grasp on her. She couldn't give in to it. "He's right." She choked out her response. "I will never marry you."

Something sparked in Micah's hazel eyes as he shot her a sideways glance. Hurt? Desperation? He leaned closer, and his hot breath seared her cheek as he whispered, "I can save *him*."

Her father, he meant. And he was right—as soon as he lowered his gun, with the help of his friends, Isaiah would regain control. The cabin would be burned—with her father and maybe herself in it, should Micah be overpowered. His fixation on her offered her the smallest leverage. She had to play along with him, at least for now. Crow and her brothers-in-law would come for them. She just needed to buy some time.

She gave the slightest dip of her head. "What do we do?"

"Everybody out." Micah waved his pistol toward the door. When the stocky man glanced at Agidoda, Micah added, "Leave the old man. We've got to get out of here before his sons show up. To the horses."

Anna's heart wrenched as Micah pushed her ahead of him, following the others out the door. A glance over her shoulder showed her father's arm spasm. Another few minutes, and he might be able to help her. But she didn't have a few minutes. Micah pulled her into the chilly night.

In a shadowy copse of trees a few hundred yards from the mill complex, her captor hefted her up onto a gray horse. She clung to the front of the saddle as he mounted behind her, ensuring she could not slip off during the journey.

Micah turned the stallion for the lane that led to the Alabama Road. The taller man rode at their side, Isaiah and the stocky man behind. Anna shot a yearning glance toward her cabin as they passed it, the welcoming lights still glowing inside. If she rode off with these men, would her future be ripped from her, never to be recovered?

Oh, God, help me.

She would throw herself from the saddle, even if it meant a broken bone. That would be better than being dishonored, held hostage, or killed.

Suddenly, she stiffened. Was that a figure darting in their direction along the darkened side of the house? A short whoop, a flash of a blade as it hurled end over end through the air, and the man riding abreast of them cried out and slumped over his horse's back.

"Crow!" Anna shrieked her brother's name.

"Go, go," Isaiah yelled behind them. His horse shot past them, frantically kicked into a canter. Clearly, he expected them to follow. His stocky comrade did so as he drew a pistol and fired behind him. The tall man jounced atop his horse as it loped along, barely clinging to the saddle. The heavy hilt of a knife protruded from his shoulder.

But Micah only trailed them a short distance, waiting until he was out of Crow's sight before he cut off through the forest. Where was he taking her? Anna grabbed the reins and pulled back on them, but one swipe of Micah's long arm—bony, but surprisingly strong—pinned her own against her sides. He wrested the leather leads from her and hissed in her ear. "No you don't, *Miss Anna*. No runnin' away this time."

Tears blurred her vision as the darkened forest swallowed them along with any chance of escape.

CHAPTER 17

Gage had to stop twice on the way to Walker Mill to cast up his accounts along the side of the road. The first time, McCleary and Ellerby reined in their mounts a dozen or so yards away and eyed him with grim concern as he resumed their ride. The second, McCleary waited until Gage sat upright and wiped his mouth to say, "Ya know we think this is an addle-pated idea. We're only along because we like Miss Anna."

"Yeah." Ellerby shifted in his saddle with a creak of leather. "No offense, but you're not worth gettin' drummed out over."

"I see you speak your mind now that I no longer outrank you." Had a threat not loomed, a chuckle might've accompanied Gage's dry observation. But for now, he'd accept the men's reason. Concern for Anna drove him as well. He'd explained what had happened earlier that day, and they'd agreed with him that only some sort of trouble at the mill—most likely, with the Thompsons—would have brought her to Fort Buffington.

As they continued east with the soft jingle of metal, the sense of foreboding only grew. Gage's head pounded in time with the horse's hooves, and the landscape blurred in and out of focus. The light of a silvery half moon illuminated the empty road before them, the bare tree branches that stretched up toward a starry sky, and the puffs of humid breath their horses expelled. Why hadn't he checked on Anna and her father before now, even if she didn't want any sort of relationship with him? Didn't he owe her that much? Wasn't that the reason he was here? Instead, he'd allowed his pride to keep him away.

They'd just turned off on Walker Lane when a pop in the distance made Gage draw up Colby's reins. Had that been musket fire? The possibility tripped his pulse like the starting shot of a race, impeding his ability to listen. But McCleary nodded at him. He'd heard it too. When no further sounds broke the silence, Gage urged his stallion ahead, the men following abreast.

Halfway to Walker Mill, hooves pounded the red clay from the opposite direction. Gage slowed Colby and held up his hand, signaling the men that they should be ready to take cover.

A familiar mare rounded a bend and galloped down an open stretch toward them—Anna's mare. But it wasn't Anna on her back. No, the figure was even smaller...a boy, slight-framed and hatless, hunched over and clinging hard. Gage's chest tightened, and he rode to meet Anna's nephew. He pulled up beside him. "Ned, what's the matter?"

"Sergeant! Am I glad to see you." The boy's obvious anxiety and quickened breathing as he straightened to shoot Gage an entreating look only raised the adolescent pitch of his voice higher. He lifted himself restlessly from the mare's back—left unsaddled in obvious haste. "They took Anna!"

Gage's heart plummeted. "Who took her?"

"Micah Thompson. He and his uncle and two other men beat up Grandfather. Hit him over the head. They were looking for gold."

"Gold!" Ellerby edged his stallion closer. "What gold?"

Gage waved his hand at him. Didn't matter. "Which way did they go?"

"You didn't see 'em?"

Gage shook his head.

"Three of 'em went that way, probably to the Thompsons' farm. First turn to the right." Ned pointed back the way they'd come. Gage and his men must've just missed them. "Father and my uncles cut through the woods to follow them, thinking they had Anna with them."

"But she wasn't?"

"No. I was going to tell my father she isn't at the Thompson place. I saw her on Micah's horse after my father and uncles left. Micah took her on a game trail, headed west."

West. What was west if the Thompsons lived to the east? And Micah had her to himself.

"Grandfather needs me. And Father needs your help with the Thompsons. You can tell him they don't have Anna. More of them will come, and my family has no guns."

Gage's head spun. His stomach clenched. He clung to Colby's sides with quivering thigh muscles. He squeezed his eyes closed in a desperate attempt to clear the fog closing in— both visual and mental.

McCleary drew near on his mount. "Sergeant...Ellerby and I must go with the boy. You, however..."

Gage was not bound by military orders to keep the peace. What bound him was his heart's tie to the woman he loved, who needed him now more than ever. "I'll go after Anna."

But how was he to find her in this vast land, and when he could barely sit a horse? He drew in an unsteady breath and straightened his shoulders. With the help of the Almighty, this last mission he would not fail.

〜

Quicksilver seemed to race through Anna's veins as Micah took one trail and backwoods lane after another. By the time he slowed his horse, she had no idea where they were. The stallion picked its way with care down a rocky hillside only weakly illuminated by the silver light of the half moon. An owl hooted from a bare branch overhead, and Anna shivered in the cool damp of the wee hours. Anxiety kept weariness at bay, sharpening her mind and senses. As they rode up to a tiny cabin nestled in the hollow, dread overtook anxiety, the happy burbling of a nearby creek a juxtaposition to the events unfolding...and completely out of her control.

Not completely. She had God, she had people who loved her who would come after her, and she had her own keen mind. She would watch for a chance of escape and defend herself using whatever means necessary. And one tool she had at her disposal was Micah's obvious need for her approval.

She dared to speak after he dismounted and reached up to help her down from his horse. "Why did you bring me here?" She slid into the circle of his arms, and when he did not immediately step back, she forced herself not to bolt. Perhaps she could reason with him. "Why not take me to your uncle's? Do you expect them to attack my family again?"

"No. They'll go home and tend to their injuries. More likely, your family will attack *them*. I want you well away from there."

Anna shrugged out of his clasp on her upper arms. "Do you forget, your people took my family's weapons away?"

A rueful chuckle rumbled from Micah's chest. "All except that musket you had hid." If she wasn't mistaken, a tinge of admiration resonated in his voice.

She lifted her chin. "And if you hadn't gotten in the way, I wouldn't have to worry about your uncle coming after us again." Despite her bravado, a secret inner relief revealed how thankful she was not to have the stain of a man's life on her soul.

"That would've been fine with me. In fact, the best outcome possible." He cocked his head as he peered at her. "It was you I was tryin' to save. Don't you know that?"

The twang of longing in his nasally voice caused confusion to spiral and words to flee, and she merely shook her head. Micah had real feelings for her, not just the drive to possess her?

"It's always been you I wanted. Why do you think I'm doin' all this? Tryin' to get this land, get you to marry me?" As he finally took a step back from her, he swept his hand out, and realization dawned.

"This is Peggy's land." And the hunting cabin where Gage had shot Isaiah.

Micah's countenance hardened. "It's *my* land. And my ticket to freedom. Once we're together, we'll have a place of respect in this community, and we can do as we please. Make a life for ourselves. And my uncle can go to the devil."

"You would really defy him?"

"When I got what I need without him, yeah. He's treated me like dirt since my pa died. Never left me a choice of whether to obey him or not, even when he asked things of me that was wrong." Memories seemed to flicker behind Micah's averted eyes, and he shifted his jaw back and forth. "It's time I became my own man."

"That's good, Micah." The man's confession softened her, and she ventured the lightest of touches to his arm, though she quickly withdrew her fingers lest he get the wrong idea. Enough of his conscience remained that she could appeal to. "You're wise to set your own course. You can start by doing the right thing now and letting me go."

Micah jerked his face in her direction. "Not if you want your father to live. No, I have to deliver what I promised." He squared his shoulders, and certainty cloaked him once more. "But don't worry. I can handle my uncle. He'll give us the time we need."

"Time we need...for what?" The last two words squeaked out of her, barely audible, as a pit opened in her stomach. Whatever Micah's feelings, his intentions could not be mistaken. Or taken lightly. He'd maneuvered himself into a corner with his family, and only one outcome would satisfy them—that they possess her land with or without her. And that made him as dangerous as his uncle.

"Time to make things official." He reached for his mount's reins and turned to lead the horse toward a rickety hitching post.

Anna took one quick look at the unfamiliar forest enclosing them on all sides. It posed less danger than the man beside her and greater chance of escape than the rutted lane that led up the hill. Without hesitating, she darted for its cover. She ran with the desperation of prey when the hunter follows close behind. And indeed, Micah's booted footsteps pounded the hard earth.

"Anna! Stop."

She plunged amongst the trees with a crunch and flurry of dry, fallen leaves and headed for an outcropping of rock where her nimble agility might outmatch his size. Her moccasins gaining purchase, she scrambled up the hillside.

She'd just reached up to maneuver around a boulder looming silver in the moonlight when hands clasped her about the waist and pulled her back. She flailed, cried out. She fell with Micah's weight pinning her beneath the rocks where windy days had swept last autumn's leaves into a rustling bed. They crackled and flew as she scrambled to escape him, but he pinned her arms and growled his displeasure.

"Fool girl. You really think I'm gonna let you get away? No. You're mine now." He lowered his head and rubbed his scratchy jaw against hers, scraping her skin and snagging strands of her hair, inhaling deeply as if taking in her scent.

Anna turned her face away. "I'll never be yours. Someone will come for me." Without weapons of their own, would Crow and her brothers-in-law send for the militia? Surely, they would. She sucked in a quick breath as hope ignited in her chest. "If the mounties learn about this, they'll take the kidnapping of a white woman very seriously. You should let me go now, while you still can. I'll not press charges." After all, Micah had gotten her away from his uncle when Isaiah would have killed her on the spot.

"I wouldn't hold out hope for that if I were you." Micah released a grim chuckle as well as her arms. "Our friend at the grocery told us them at the fort sent for a doctor this afternoon. Measles outbreak. And your precious sergeant was the first one down. He can't walk, much less ride, so he won't be comin' for you." He rolled onto his knees, then came to his feet. He extended his hand to help her up, but Anna lay there, as stunned as if she'd fallen from a height and had the wind knocked out of her.

Measles? Gage? That was why he'd run from her earlier today. Not because he didn't want to see her, but because he wanted to protect her...as he always had. Peggy had been correct, and Anna had been a fool. And now she might never have the chance to put things right. By the time Gage learned of her abduction, she'd most likely be ruined. Those in Oklahoma Territory might never know what happened here tonight, but to a white man like Gage from a good family, reputation would matter. Purity would matter.

She sat up and scooted away from Micah's outstretched hand. "I'll never enter that cabin willingly with you, and I'll never marry you. Even if you dishonor me. I'd sooner let the lottery winner have my land."

Micah's features darkened. "Have it your way." Quick as a

snake striking, he grabbed her wrists, hauling her up against him. With a groan, he smashed his lips to hers, grinding his mouth against hers with enough force to drive her lips into her teeth.

She cried out and shoved him, but he kept her pinned against his chest, nuzzling his face into her neck and hair.

"Oh, Anna, all along, I only wished you'd choose me."

His words sent a chill down her body. Hadn't she felt a similar desperation to be chosen? What a dangerous road that could lead one down. She swallowed and spoke past the bitterness that rose at his mistreatment of her. "All we need is for God to choose us, Micah. And He does."

He lifted his head, and his eyes blazed in the moonlight. "That's not enough. I want you. And I will have you, one way or another. You decide which way, and decide by dawn, or my uncle will bring the entire Pony Club against your family. Then it won't be only your land you'll lose."

The fight drained from Anna, and an invisible weight bent her head and shoulders forward. *Oh God, help me.* She might stand against Micah's demands while it was only her honor and her future at stake, but the lives of her family...? Her precious father, who loved her more than her birth father ever had? Her brave brother, who should have lived as a warrior, proud and free, a hundred years ago? Her sweet, trusting Ned with his bright mind and whole life in front of him? How could she sacrifice them to save herself?

Despair closed around her as her captor shoved her ahead of him to the cabin.

CHAPTER 18

The game trail Micah Thompson had taken had long ago branched into two, then three options before spilling out on a country lane, only to resume a hundred yards down the way. At each juncture, Gage had dismounted despite the clenching of his stomach and spinning of head and knelt to study the ground to the best of his ability. But he was no tracker, and the half moon provided insufficient illumination. The truth was, they could've gone any which way. He might as well be chasing thistledown in a hurricane.

He straightened and let out a groan. After he uncorked his canteen and took a tentative sip, he tilted his head skyward and sent a prayer up toward the stars. *God, please help me. I cannot fail this time. But I can't do this on my own.*

He might not be a soldier, but he still had a mission to fulfill here, and the loss of Anna only served to confirm that she was part of it. Fear and love tangled in a knot so painful, it burned in his chest. He couldn't lose her. To her own choice, yes. That was hers to make. But not to a scoundrel like Micah Thompson...and all he represented. Greedy settlers who took what they wanted with no thought to others.

Greedy settlers who wanted...land. Gage coughed out a breath as the idea clicked into place. *Thank You, Lord.*

He climbed back onto Colby and gathered the reins. Where would Micah take Anna but to the land he wanted to claim with her by his side? Gage might not find Mrs. Campbell's hunting cabin by the trails and back lanes Micah had, but he could bet this lane fed back into Alabama Road, and he could ride straight to it from there.

Colby's hooves beat the red clay as Gage made haste in the moonlight. The drumming sound and his intense focus caused him to miss the thunder of someone approaching from behind until the dark horse and rider were almost upon him. Gage whipped his pistol from his belt and swung it toward the man's chest.

"Whoa!" One of the newcomer's hands shot up. "I'm here to help. Don't shoot me, soldier boy."

Gage pulled back on his reins, turning Colby in a circle while he peered at the other rider. Foekiller? Uh... "Smoke Sanders?" It was definitely him, his long hair in two braids beneath his slouch hat, his buckskin hunting shirt gleaming in the moonlight, though no bow and arrows rode his back now. The militia had taken even those away. "What are you doing here?"

"Ned came to get my family after he talked to you. He figured his father and uncles could use more help against the Thompsons...in case your mounties can't stop a fight." Smoke removed his hat and swiped his forehead, which must be damp despite the chilly night. "More of my people have weapons hidden than your army knows."

That didn't surprise him a bit. Gage might have returned the man's grin if the situation had not been so dire. "Not my army anymore."

"I heard. And so I can stand the thought of helping you rescue Anna. Seems you need me more than they do."

Any urge to grin withered away, and Gage sat straighter in the saddle. "She's not yours, you know. Even if you do this."

"I know." Smoke's dark brows slanted downward. "But she is a good woman, better than I deserved, and I have a score to settle with Micah Thompson."

Gage rubbed his jaw a moment before answering. "Fine. Do you have a weapon?"

Smoke lifted a beaded sheath with a bone handle sticking out of it and dangling from a leather thong on his neck.

"Little good that will do against a musket."

"Do not be so sure. I prefer up close and personal. And I never run from a fight." The deadpan way the man spoke the words and the glitter in his eyes left no doubt of his sincerity.

Gage grimaced. "Fine, but only if you wait to go in at my command." He couldn't have unexpected heroics ruining a sound plan. Which he didn't have yet. But once he assessed the situation, with God's help, he would. Who would have thought he'd ever have fought alongside this man? Yet he was in no position to turn down an offer of help, and who was to say the proud warrior hadn't been sent by the Almighty Himself?

Smoke gave a single nod.

"All right." They'd already wasted too much time talking...time Micah could be having his way with Anna. No...Gage couldn't think about that, or he'd lose focus. "Let's go."

They urged their horses forward. Soon enough, they were turning off the road and galloping through Mrs. Campbell's field. They picketed the stallions in the same place Gage had left them the day he shot Isaiah, before adding powder to his pistol and musket. Since the weapons belonged to him, he'd kept both after leaving the militia. He glanced up to find Smoke staring at him with obsidian eyes.

"How do I know I can trust you?" Gage spoke the question uppermost in his mind.

"How much do you love Anna Walker?"

Only a beat of time and Gage asked, "You as accurate with a musket as you are with a bow and arrow?"

Smoke's teeth flashed white in the moonlight. "Better."

With a disbelieving grunt and more than a little apprehension, Gage handed Smoke the larger weapon, followed by a handful of pre-wrapped powder and ammunition. "Only fire if necessary," he said as Smoke tucked the shot away in his bandolier bag. "And only once Anna is well clear." Gage secured the pistol in his belt. If necessary, he planned to be the one to get up close and personal.

"I'm no fool. I have no wish to go before a judge again."

The grim statement brought Gage's own predicament into sharper relief. He no longer wielded the authority or enjoyed the protection of the military. Should this go poorly, he could end up in as much trouble as Smoke. But ever since the answer to his prayer directing him here, his headache and nausea had cleared, replaced by keen clarity and a determination he'd never felt before. Today his mission was personal. Too much was at stake not to succeed. He'd do what he must to free Anna and worry about repercussions later. He'd gladly face a military tribunal if it meant keeping her safe.

Dry leaves sliding under his boots, Gage led the way down the hill to observe the cabin from the familiar boulder. The faint burble of the creek created a misleading peaceful melody. A horse stood with head and ears lowered, secured to a hitching post. The single window was shuttered, but light flickered around the edges. His pulse picked up. Anna was inside. But how was he to get her out without endangering her? A man as desperate as Micah would not hesitate to hold her hostage if it came to bargaining for his own life. They had to find a way to get Anna away from him prior to any potential confrontation.

Gage made himself sit back and draw deep breaths until logic could overpower the powerful instinct to charge the front door. That would not work here any more than it worked...

In Florida.

A distraction. That was what he needed. Could he use the very thing that had foiled him before to save Anna now?

Perhaps not him, but...

Gage turned to Smoke. "Any chance you can sound like a panther?"

The Cherokee man stared at him a moment before giving a nod. To his credit, he did not waste time with unnecessary questions.

Gage could only pray Anna would remember the story he'd told her the day he'd been wounded at the mill and know what to do. This tiny cabin had no rear door, but hopefully... "If you can get him out on the porch, Anna may have a chance to get away. You stay here. I'm going to circle around the back to that stand of cane near the creek. Give me five minutes to get in position. Don't go in unless I whistle."

Smoke's ambivalent expression suggested his plan might have differed significantly from Gage's, but again, the man did not argue. He merely positioned himself behind the boulder and rested the gun barrel on the granite. The musket looked right in his hands.

An unexpected rush of nostalgia flooded Gage. Him going into action alongside a Cherokee? Father would be proud.

Gage set off through the woods, walking as softly as his father had taught him, who'd learned from his grandfather. The man who had not been loyal to his country but who had loved the Cherokee people. Funny how that all came into play in this pivotal moment.

Gage had just taken position in the edge of the canebrake when a loud chirp from near the boulder made him stiffen and suck in a breath. What was Smoke doing?

Of course...a panther didn't just scream. It made a variety of noises, and that one was convincing enough without being overly threatening that the front door of the cabin opened.

Micah was coming out to see if he'd heard what he thought he did. But would Anna be ready when Smoke gave the signal? Was she even able to move?

Gage's stomach clenched. He had failed to consider that she might be tied up...or worse.

~

The strange sound from the wooded hill facing the cabin brought Anna's head up from where she had rested it on her bound hands in a posture of prayer. And not just a posture—though doubtless, her demeanor bought her some time with Micah. She'd told him she needed a long talk with the Lord if Micah didn't want her to hate him for the rest of her life. In truth, she clung to the hope that her family would come for her...maybe with the militia. At least the scrap of decency Micah retained made him willing to wait and see if she'd wed him without him forcing himself upon her.

He had dozed while she travailed in prayer, but he sat on the floor with his back against the door, his musket in his arms. Clearly, the stress of the prior day had taken its toll on him. Just not enough to render him harmless. The one time she had risen from her chair, thinking she would inspect the single window as a possible means of escape, he'd flashed to alertness and waved her back to her seat. "Dawn," he'd said.

Apparently, at that dreaded hour, she either agreed to call the preacher or he'd see that she would. Not much to ponder there. And certainly, if he rode for a preacher, she had a chance of escape. But she'd wait to render her verdict until the last possible moment.

"What was that?" Anna held her breath, listening, but Micah scrambled up.

"Sounded like a panther."

A chill ran down her arms. "That strange little croak?"

"They make all kinds of noises." He rested his hand on the bolt over the door, then withdrew it. "Or it could be that someone's out there. Either way, best stay inside."

Anna sat upright. "The cat could've come out of the canebrake. What if it attacks your horse? You left the poor thing tied up. Then you couldn't ride for the preacher."

He leveled a look at her. "Is that what you decided?"

She raised her chin. "Seems to me you're going to get what you want either way. Might as well be proper-like. But you can't go if the horse is mauled." Was it horribly wrong of her to hope there *was* a panther, and that if it attacked, it might give her the chance to escape?

His eyes had sparked and widened when she spoke of her decision, but then the corners of his mouth drew flat. "Don't make sense for no panther to be out in this warm—"

A guttural cry tore into the end of his sentence.

Anna shot to her feet. Chill bumps rippled down her arms, and her pulse raced. Her mind as well. For the last time someone had spoken of a panther came back to her. Gage. He'd told of the Seminole scout in Florida who had signaled the youths to flee from the cabin the militia had surrounded. Could it be? Was he out there? Hope slammed into her heart and pumped it hard. "It's closer. You must shoot it!"

"Stay back." Micah jerked the door open and swept the gun barrel from one end of the yard to the other. "There's somethin' on the hill." The musket strap flapped as he snatched the weapon upward. He took a couple steps onto the porch.

Unlike in Gage's story, this cabin had no rear door, and the only window faced forward. Anna had one way to flee—right past Micah. If she didn't want him to stop her, she had to knock him down. The drop from the porch ought to do. So long as he couldn't grab or shoot her, she'd take her chances with whatever fate awaited her in the woods.

She raised her bound hands to her chest and launched

herself forward as hard and fast as she could. As her footsteps thudded across the dirt floor, Micah turned toward her and lowered the loaded weapon, his eyes going wide.

A shot rang out from the woods facing the cabin.

Micah's hat flew off. Carried by momentum, she plowed into him. They tumbled off the porch. Unable to break her fall with her arms, Anna landed on the leg she'd injured when seeking to escape him before. Her ankle twisted with a hot, searing pain. A cry left her lips.

But she couldn't stop. Somehow Micah had retained hold of his gun. She pulled herself to her feet and hobbled a few steps toward the woods...toward either the arms of her savior or the claws of a panther.

"Anna!"

Gage! The sheer terror in his voice whipped her head around. From where he stood at the rear corner of the cabin, he raised a pistol. Only then did she realize Micah had pointed his musket at her. Alerted by Gage's cry, Micah swung it toward the new threat. If she didn't intervene, he could pull the trigger before Gage could take aim.

Once again, she threw herself at her captor. Micah's musket flashed in the dark, filling her ears with a roar and ringing. She crumpled atop his side as he landed with a thud.

Booted steps ran toward them. Micah rolled into a crouch. Anna fought to right herself as he groped for her.

A trigger clicked. "Hands up."

Micah froze but did not comply.

"Hands up now, or I shoot them off like I meant to do your uncle's." Gage loomed over them, face pale in the moonlight, his pistol trained on Micah.

"Better yet, I put a hole through his head rather than his hat this time." Another man rounded the front side of the cabin, a musket aimed at his foe on the ground. "Which I would have done if he hadn't turned around."

Anna blinked. Smoke Sanders? The last person she would've expected to see with Gage.

Micah released her and raised both hands—the far one from the top of his boot, where the long handle of a knife protruded. Anna gasped. Had Gage been a second later, Micah would have held the blade to her throat. She wasted no time in grasping the hand Gage held out to her. He slid her behind him, keeping his pistol at the ready until Smoke had disarmed Micah and wrestled him to the ground.

The Cherokee man planted a moccasin on Micah's back. "I need something to tie him."

"Can you use this rope?" Anna stepped around Gage and raised her bound hands. His look of compassion melted her heart.

He made quick work of the knots and tossed the rope to Smoke. Only when Micah was secured did Gage gently encircle her wrists, skimming the chafe marks with a feather-soft touch. He lifted his eyes to hers. "Did he harm you?" When she shook her head, he raised his brows, not breaking the gaze. "You can tell the truth, Anna. It won't make any difference...except I might kill him here." He growled out the last.

"You came in time. Truly. But how did you know?"

"Your nephew—he saw which way Micah took you and rode your mare to find me."

"Poor Ned. He must've flown like lightning." Though she spoke fondly of the boy, it was the man before her for whom love swelled in her breast. She brushed back a wave of brown hair that escaped Gage's hat and stuck to his forehead. Her fingers came away clammy.

"I was already on my way."

Anna blinked at him. "You were? But why?"

"I couldn't have you thinking I avoided you. Or that I was drunk." And yet he swayed ever so slightly as he spoke.

Oh, but... "You were sick." Alarm lanced through her, and

she braced his shoulders. "Measles! Micah said there was an outbreak." The man's grumbling and cursing as Smoke tightened the rope around his wrists barely registered for Anna. The attack on Agidoda, her abduction—the terror of recent events had erased all else from her mind for a time...as the man before her did now. "And yet you came for me."

"Of course, I came for you." There was no mistaking the tenderness in his expression. Nevertheless, he took a step back. "It isn't measles as we first thought when you came to the fort, but you still shouldn't be close to me."

"I don't care." Anna's chest flooded with warmth, and she flung her arms around his neck and pressed the side of her face against his coat, inhaling the spicy scent of wool and man. "There's so much I have to tell you." She hadn't even gotten the chance to relay the request from the Red Bank tribe that had taken her to the fort in the first place, though it now seemed long ago that she had learned of it herself.

A throat clearing reminded her they were not alone, and they broke apart. Smoke shifted his weight, his musket still pointed at Micah, who lay prone on the ground with his hands tied behind his back. "If you lovebirds don't mind, I could use some help getting this *i-na-dv* on a horse."

Gage offered a regretful smile and a quick squeeze of her hand before he went to assist.

Anna watched with a painful pull in her chest. Peggy's words couldn't have proven truer, for Anna no longer wondered what she would give up if she found real love. But after all her inconsistency, would Gage still want her? Especially once he learned she had sought him out after being charged with the sacred trust of guarding the Red Bank gold?

CHAPTER 19

$\mathcal{A}$nna should have ridden behind Gage on his stallion, not the other way around. By the time they approached the turn to Walker Lane, she pretty well supported his weight as he slumped against her. Her lack of a wrap no longer made a difference, for the furnace-like heat radiating from his body kept her warm.

She swiveled to speak to him. "You should have let me stay with Peggy as I suggested."

Whatever energy the search for her had roused in him had clearly ebbed by the time Anna accompanied Gage and Smoke into Fort Buffington. On the ride there, the two men had harassed each other like boyhood friends about the ways each could have carried out her rescue better. Anna had owned her part in running toward the panther cry rather than behind the cabin as Gage had hoped she'd remember to do. In truth, that the whole thing had worked had been nothing short of a miracle.

Once they had delivered a dejected and sullen Micah to Gage's former lieutenant, Gage looked ready to drop. No doubt, he longed for nothing more than his own cot. Yet he had only waited long enough to give a brief report and for the officer to dispatch a contingent of mounties to the Thompson place before insisting on taking Anna home.

With a rumble of protest, he made an effort to straighten. "I told you—I'm not letting your father worry about you one extra minute, nor you about him."

"You're right. I am worried. But he was starting to stir when Micah took me from the cabin." Anna quelled a swell of misgiving. Just because he awoke did not mean all would be well. Look at the effects of a blow to the head Gage had suffered. How much worse might it damage an older man? "I should be there to tend him. And you."

"Not me. I won't expose you to this sickness more than I have to. We don't know what it is yet."

"Nonsense. I am not afraid of a fever." She was much more concerned about what it might do to him in her absence. He would not receive the care he needed, for the new doctor still had not returned to the fort, and the one in Canton had his hands full with a measles outbreak. "You are not going anywhere this day. We will make a pallet by the fire as we did before." To emphasize her words, she took the reins from his slack hands.

Another question raised anxiety, though she did not voice it to Gage, as he had likely already considered it. What had happened when her family members had surrounded the Thompsons' homestead? Had the militia arrived in time to de-escalate a conflict? Or might there be wounded...or dead... waiting at her cabin in more dire need of her ministrations than even her father or Gage?

Dread gripped her insides. Too much time had passed. The faint light of dawn already touched the horizon with a golden glow. Everything in her urged her to speed up, but she now secured Gage's hand in place at her waist. It was unlikely he could hold on at a canter.

As they approached the wooded turnoff to Walker Lane, a dozen or more riders materialized from the trees and spilled onto the main road. Anna's heart jumped, and Gage came to attention behind her, his free hand reaching for his pistol.

"Edmonds!" The brogue detectable even in the speaking of the name allowed Anna to expel the breath she'd sucked in.

Behind her, Gage relaxed, releasing his weapon and reaching around her to take back the reins. "Private McCleary. I'm very glad it's you."

The Scotsman's bulky form came into focus as he detached from where he rode at the head of the group and urged his horse forward to meet them. "I canna say but I feel the same about you. And especially about her." His teeth flashed in the pale light as he took stock of her riding before Gage. "Evenin', Miss Walker. Or should I say, mornin'?"

Anna returned his nod of recognition. "Good morning."

"I shoulda known you'd bring her back." McCleary winked at Gage.

"Or die trying." The deep rumble of conviction in Gage's statement made her stomach flip over. "Looks like you got your men too."

The other riders became distinguishable in the faint light as they drew to a halt about ten yards away. An escort comprised of unfamiliar mounties surrounded Isaiah Thompson and his two friends. Luke Ellerby brought up the rear. Anna took in a slow, shaky breath as relief flooded her. Isaiah would bother them no more...at least for now.

The bound hands and the strain of pain on the faces of Isaiah, his arm wrapped with a stained bandage, and the other man who'd taken the knife to the back made the glares they sent Anna's way less lethal. Nevertheless, Gage's arm around her tightened, and he kept his other hand near his pistol. That he would protect her even when weakened by illness brought a sweet ache to her chest.

"Yeah." McCleary shifted in the saddle and tipped his hat back. "By the time Ellerby and I got there, we had a standoff on our hands. One of Miss Walker's relatives had fired a warnin' shot to let the Thompsons know they meant business. They called out demandin' Miss Walker's return. They wouldna believe Isaiah here didna have her." He gestured to the sullen man behind him. "They woulda stormed the cabin despite our warnin' against it if you hadna sent these men from Buffington."

Anna could stand the suspense no longer. She leaned over Coby's neck. "So no one was hurt?"

"That's right." Another soldier with broad shoulders and a deep voice spoke from behind McCleary.

"Thank God." Anna breathed out the words and sagged a little. Crow and her brothers-in-law were alive, unharmed.

"Sergeant Moss, ma'am." He tipped his hat at her. "Once Thompson realized he was not only surrounded but also outnumbered, he and his friends surrendered, and we were able to search the premises. We're taking them back to Fort Buffington for medical care, where they'll stand trial for assault and kidnapping."

She swallowed and spoke low enough that she hoped Isaiah Thompson would not hear. "So they'll not go free?"

"They'll not see the outside of a jail cell for quite some time, miss."

A shudder shook her. "Quite some time isn't enough."

Gage ran his hand along her arm and murmured in her ear. "It's enough for now."

He was right. She needed to get home to her father. How anxious he must be—assuming he was alert. Anna tipped her head forward. "Thank you, Sergeant."

"We're only glad you're all right, ma'am. This could've ended badly, indeed."

Yes. With her dishonored and shackled to an unbalanced

and abusive man, her relatives wounded or killed on her behalf, and open war declared between the Cherokees and the Pony Club—a conflict that would have also drawn in the military. Truly, they owed deep gratitude to God that the worst had been avoided.

Anna offered a quavering smile to the Scotsman whose silence deferred to his superior. "Thank you, Private McCleary." She broadened her gaze to include all the mounties. "And all of you."

As the soldiers murmured a response and resumed their ride toward Buffington, Gage's friend lifted a hand in farewell, reins threaded through his gloved fingers. His big stallion skittered sideways, and he once again melted into the group. The thud of hooves and jingle of harnesses faded, replaced by the soft brush of a chilly morning breeze and the twitter of a bird heralding the new day.

Anna expected Gage to urge Colby forward, but his arms firmed around her instead. He lowered his face to the back of her neck and murmured, "Don't be afraid, Anna."

In response to his hot breath on her skin and how well he read her misgivings, a tremble ran through her. "How can I not be? It feels as though we cannot win, even when these men commit crimes against us."

Gage lifted his head and spoke firmly. "Though I'm not officially part of the army now, I'm not without influence, and I'll do everything in my power to ensure that justice is served."

"But for how long? If the Thompsons remain, their position will only be strengthened by the gain of Peggy's property. And mine will be diminished by the removal of my family." The unswerving allegiance and fierce protection of her adoptive father and half brother had insulated her from harm for so long, she couldn't imagine the pain the lack of it would bring. And so well that she couldn't imagine its replacement. Certainly, no birth family could have done more. And still, trusting the word and the intentions of a single man made her so vulnerable.

As what she said registered, Gage sucked in a soft breath. "Does that mean you want to stay?"

She froze for a moment, her heart skipping a beat. "Do you still want me to?" She swiveled to face him, seeking to read his expression. Hope? Her heart thundered like a runaway wagon.

"More than anything."

Anna placed her hand on his chest. "Do not speak too soon. As I said at the cabin, there is more I need to tell you. If I stay, it will be with a responsibility that may continue to bring danger."

"I don't care what it is." Gage cupped the side of her face, and Colby shifted as the reins went slack. "Whatever it is, wherever it is—here or in Oklahoma—let me be by your side."

A spasm of joy bolted through her. "Do you mean that?"

"It's the one thing I know for sure. I love you, Anna." His arm tightened around her with emphasis.

Shaking her head in amazement, Anna caressed his lightly whiskered jaw. "I love you, too, Gage." She leaned in, and when he made a sound of protest, she only drew him closer and pressed her lips against his, once, then twice—a testament that, unlike their last kiss, she chose it. Chose him. She pulled back with a soft laugh. "Some things are more important than a fever." Besides, soon enough, she would employ the contents of her herb box to the best of her ability.

Gage didn't so much as pause before speaking again. "Such as the fact that if you'll have me, I want nothing more than to marry you?"

"Yes. I want that too." Overcome with emotion, she cradled his face with both hands. Moved closer to kiss him again. "Let's go home. There, we will set all things right."

Gage nodded and drew in the reins, calling to Colby. They

shot forward as the first rays of sun bathed the land in golden promise.

There would be pain in her future. But now she also knew there would be joy.

~

*P*urple violets dotted the carpet of brown leaves at the edge of the woods as Gage followed Anna and her father up the same path where she'd cut honeysuckle vines last November. Early March had brought buds to the trees. Vegetation greened beside the burbling creek. Robins darted about in search of worms, and jonquils nodded their creamy and golden heads in the rills and nooks of the forest.

Three days had passed since Gage brought Anna home from Mrs. Campbell's hunting cabin. When Ned had bounded across the yard calling Anna's name and thrown himself into her arms, and then her father and half brother had come out onto the porch, the joy that had flooded Gage at Anna's declaration of love had multiplied tenfold. For he'd finally accomplished something truly meaningful. And according to Anna, today he could choose whether or not to serve her people in a new way, one she had kept strangely quiet about while she nursed him through his fever. Today had been the first day he'd ventured out of their cabin.

Where were they taking him?

When they came to the boulder where Gage and Anna had watched the two Cherokee men carve the strange symbol, Joshua nimbly crossed the creek on a trail of dry stones, giving no sign of ill effects from the blow to his head. Anna had stayed after him with her herbs and concoctions as diligently as she had Gage, until both men groaned about her bitter potions. Though they bolted them down with grins that followed the grimaces.

Unlike her father, Anna turned back with a come-on gesture and a dimpled smile that made Gage long to sweep her into his arms and sneak a kiss when Joshua wasn't looking. A real kiss. Despite the pleasure Joshua couldn't quite hide when they'd told him about their engagement, the man hadn't left them alone for two minutes together. The better Gage felt, the more of a trial that became. He'd apply to Joshua again about getting a preacher to the house as soon as possible. Once one knew what he wanted, the only effect of dragging things out was the pain of separation, and Gage had no intention of allowing that to set in. He would only go back to the fort to serve out his term once Anna was his wife.

And yet she had refrained from speaking of their future since their return to her home. When he'd brought it up, she'd told him to wait. That she had something to show him, and only afterward could they make plans. Even now, a certain intensity energized her, as though her muscles coiled tight. She leapt over every other stone her father had stepped on and looked back to make certain he followed. With less agility, Gage did.

The next stretch of ground they covered more resembled a game trail than a path. An abundance of roots and rocks forced one to watch the ground to avoid missteps. Eventually, they left even the trail and climbed a ridge overlooking the creek. They'd just come to a level spot on pebbled soil when a flash of movement ahead jangled alarm through Gage. A woman stepped from behind a boulder in what seemed to be a den of similarly sized rocks.

"Mrs. Campbell!"

The innkeeper wore a drab brown dress in a simpler style than Gage had ever seen her in before. "Hello, Gage." She greeted him as her husband appeared behind her, holding a lit lantern. What was this?

And which was more startling, her sudden appearance in

the middle of the forest or her calling him by his first name? Clearly, she knew more than he did about this outing.

Gage turned to Anna, who had stopped beside him, her breathing slightly faster from the climb. "What's going on here?"

"We want to show you something." Gesturing for him to follow, Anna approached the den from which her friends had emerged...which turned out to be a small cave. Gage halted to examine it, forcing Joshua to draw up abruptly behind him.

Anna's father tilted his head toward the darkened opening. "Go in."

Gage had to duck to enter the passageway running between two boulders. He expected it to peter out, but instead, after about twenty yards, it opened into a small, rounded chamber. The dank air felt colder here. Mrs. Campbell and Anna followed him in, while Joshua stood in the entrance to the room holding the lantern aloft, and Mr. Hummingbird waited outside—almost as if standing guard.

That seemed even more a possibility when Joshua pointed upward to where another large stone crowned a channel that ran at a diagonal angle toward the doorway. "There will be a deadfall to secure the opening once everything is prepared."

A deadfall? Gage frowned, searching for the trigger mechanism, which apparently had not been installed yet.

Mrs. Campbell crossed to the far side of the wall. She pulled a thin-bladed knife from a sheath at her waist and wedged it into the rock about shoulder high. When a slab of granite slid outward, allowing her to grasp and remove it, Gage blinked in surprise. She set the square slice of rock at her feet and reached into the opening. A moment later, she faced him holding a lidded clay pot—in her arms, not her hands, which meant its weight must have been considerable.

"Open it," she bade him.

He did so and let out a huff of breath. "What is this?" Inside the pottery, jewelry and gold coins nestled in a bed of fine gold dust.

"These, my good young man, are all the worldly goods my husband and I possess apart from our home. But the government will not allow us to take them to Oklahoma Territory." Regret thickened Mrs. Campbell's voice as she stared at her family heirlooms.

"So you're leaving them here."

"Yes." The woman shifted the clay pot to her side as she answered. "There will be two dozen deposits like this from our tribe alone, not just in this cave, but in others, along the creek bank, and at the foot of marker trees."

Gage swung his gaze to Anna, who returned it soberly. "The day we found the men engraving the boulder," he said, "you were right—they were making a map on the land."

"A treasure map."

Her father stepped forward, the circle of light from the lantern he held growing with him. "There will be a printed map as well, one that will be delivered once they receive our assurance that Anna will stay. Should spoken directions fail, it will make certain that the location of any treasure is not lost to time. The journey will take many months, and we do not know how long it will be before it will be safe to return."

Frustration mounting at the injustice of it all, Gage turned back to Mrs. Campbell. "Will you not fight this? I received a reply from my captain stating that he plans to ensure that the Thompsons do not get your land. Not after what they've done."

"As thankful as I am to hear that, it does not change the eventual outcome." She gestured with her chin for Gage to return the lid to the pot. Once she had secured her heavy burden inside the compartment carved to contain an object of its exact size, she sighed and met his gaze. "Unlike Anna, I do not have the option to marry to maintain my holdings. Nor would I change that if I could." She glanced toward the opening of the tunnel, to where her husband waited outside. "Whither he goest, I will go."

When Anna stepped closer and slid her cool, slender hand into Gage's, his heart warmed. He squeezed her fingers. "I understand."

A brief smile softened Mrs. Campbell's face. "Anna told me you were willing even to accompany her to Oklahoma." She bent to retrieve the vault's door slab, then straightened and looked at him again, firmly this time. "Which is why I'm hoping you'll understand what has been asked of her."

"You want her to stay and help safeguard your treasure." He spoke with certainty, not needing to look at Anna to confirm the truth.

"Not just I. Anna has been asked by the chief of the Red Bank tribe to remain at Walker Mill, to be the caretaker of our worldly goods until we can return to claim them."

Gage did look at Anna then. She nodded and said, "The two men we saw that day along the creek, Yousannah and Arch, paid us a visit. It's why I was coming to the fort last week. They did not only ask about me. You are trusted and respected by the tribe. They believe that together, we can watch over that which is too valuable for them to take on their journey."

He took a step back, her fingers falling from his grasp. "They said that?"

"Yes." A frown flitted between her brows. "Why do you find that hard to believe?"

"I had no idea..." Gage rubbed his jaw. "No indication they even knew who I was, much less that they would trust me with such an important task." Humility and gratitude brought a sheen of tears to his eyes, and he stared at the cave's sandy floor to hide his unwelcome emotion. Somehow, the regard of the people he'd come to serve salved the wound of his father's disappointment in him. If he did this, would his father not be proud? Would Gage not finally even the scales?

She drew closer to him, brushing against his side as she clasped his arm. "You have been true to your convictions. Everyone knows what kind of man you are, Gage."

He covered her hand with his and managed a smile. "What is most important is that you know."

"I do." She squeezed his arm. "Which is why I'm asking if you'll accept this responsibility with me. You see, as much as it breaks my heart to be parted from my family, I've decided this is the way I can serve my people best."

Gage nodded. Swallowed. "Then it's the way I can serve them...and you...best as well."

"There may be danger." The breathless, hopeful way she delivered the warning rendered it almost powerless in Gage's mind.

"Bring it on." He flashed her a grin, a confidence filling him he'd never felt before. "Everything makes sense now—all the things that have gone before. God was preparing me, preparing *us*, for this moment. This is what I was meant to do all along. As your husband."

The adoring look Anna bestowed upon him settled the matter of taking her into his arms.

Her father harrumphed, but Mrs. Campbell turned from securing her treasure with a clap of her hands that suited her normally buoyant nature. "Then it's decided. Come, Joshua, let us return to the house, and George and I will fetch the preacher." Not giving Anna's father a chance to argue, she hooked her arm through his and drew him into the light.

Bless the woman. Gage could finally kiss his sweetheart properly. But first, he raised a brow and asked, "How do you feel about becoming a bride today?"

Anna's smile left him dazzled. "Bring it on."

The sweet press of her lips against his promised joy and purpose for the rest of their days.

EPILOGUE

June 1842

God had taken His paintbrush to Eastern Oklahoma. Anna couldn't stop marveling over the array of vivid colors as Gage drove their wagon south of Tahlequah. On this bright June morning, she would see her family again for the first time in four years. The rolling green hills surrounding the new Cherokee capital, cradled in the foothills of the Ozarks, took her by surprise. She had expected flat plains. Rocky, arid landscapes. Had anticipated that the descriptions Peggy and her family sent had been enhanced to spare her worry. How glad she was that her people had a beautiful land not so vastly different from their beloved Appalachians to call their new home.

Fields of red Indian Blankets blooming along the Illinois River stole her breath. Bees and hummingbirds buzzed among the white blossoms on buttonbush and massive silver linden trees with their fluttering leaves, dark green on top and almost metallic-looking on bottom. Their three-year-old son, named for both of their fathers, Joshua Garrison Edmonds, declared from the wagon seat between them that the yellow coneflowers with their brown tops and droopy yellow petals looked like ladies in bonnets and bright skirts.

He was always saying things like that, his observations delivered in a serious tone with his hat tipped over his face, his hands stuffed in his pockets, and his shoulders hunched casually forward in the posture of a wizened little man. He needed only a corncob pipe or toothpick to complete the picture.

Really, his precociousness should come as no surprise, as he spent his days at home following her and Gage about in the woods, fields, and grindstone. Regular mill customers would stop in just to chat with the tyke and laugh at the adult-sounding things he said. It would be good for him to spend time with other children, his cousins.

"Not long now." Gage offered her a smile as he kept the horses to a pace meant to not jostle her overmuch on the drive to Goingsnake Creek where the Walkers had settled. "You holding up all right?"

His never-ending concern for her warmed her heart. It seemed they grew closer every year—maybe because they had only each other to lean on. While Gage's mother and sisters had embraced Anna after their marriage in April of 1838, the demands of the mill and distance to Gainesville meant their visits were sporadic at best. Though Anna suspected she'd be seeing more of them upon their return to Georgia, especially if this new baby she carried was a girl. Her pregnancy had come as a welcome surprise—if somewhat inconvenient, due to the fact that they'd been traveling since late March. Anna would not protest the timing, however, for she had begun to wonder if she'd be able to conceive another child.

"I'm fine." The wink she gave Gage drew him closer for a quick kiss over Josh's head.

"I know this trip has been hard on you, though you've not uttered a complaint."

Anna shrugged. "A little nausea is nothing to complain about. Especially when I consider what my family endured to get here."

She needn't say more for Gage's countenance to cloud. They didn't speak of the Trail of Tears, *nu na da ul tsun yi*, where four thousand Cherokees had died of cold, starvation, and disease on their eight-hundred-mile journey to Oklahoma, on foot, between November 1838 and March 1839. The dark days had begun even before that, when troops began rounding up Cherokee families in their area after the May 23 deadline. Thankfully, Gage's term as interpreter had ended a couple of weeks before, but it had broken their hearts when Anna's family had walked into Fort Buffington and the gate had closed behind them.

Others had not gone so peacefully. Some soldiers had obeyed General Winfield Scott's directive to not separate families and to remove the people with "every possible kindness." Other members of the militia exerted their authority and prejudice with cruelty. By May 28, Captain Buffington presided over four hundred Cherokees in the small enclosure. Word came that some Cherokees escaped to the hills, and around a thousand of their people who lived on private land in North Carolina were allowed to remain.

Anna had visited her father and half siblings and their children until Captain Buffington heeded his superiors' demands that he move the Cherokees under his command on June 9. She had not been able to bring herself to visit Buffington when the 479 prisoners interred there left for Ross's Landing and the west but instead had said her tearful goodbyes the day prior.

It had taken months for her to rise above the grief that followed. Her new husband had proven unfailingly patient with her. Gage's love and the birth of their first child had pulled her from despair. And gradually, she began to build her new life, making some cherished friendships, especially with the mixed-blood families allowed to remain because the head of household was white. The mill had become a gathering place where the Cherokee language and traditions were remembered and observed.

Finally, though, the rare letters from Oklahoma had not been enough to assuage Anna's longing for her family. Preparing for such a lengthy trip meant Gage had needed to train an apprentice to the point he would be competent to oversee the fall harvest on his own. Originally, they'd meant to return by January, but with the new little one due in November, they would now extend their stay to spring.

Anna focused on the positive. "I'm glad we'll get more time than expected with my family. You can help Agidoda with the mill, and I will have plenty of time to prepare for the baby."

"I don't know how much help I'll be. From your father's letters, it sounds as though Ned has just about taken over. But I was encouraged by how Tahlequah is growing. Especially that they have a doctor." He shot her a smile.

They had stayed at the new capital the night before, coming in late on the main highway from Fort Smith on the Arkansas border. Four stores and a number of houses had surrounded Tahlequah's log-and-frame government complex, though they'd needed to find lodging in a home with a room off the back porch for travelers since there was no inn yet. Hopefully, the treasure they concealed in the wagon bed would help change that.

Suddenly, Josh sat up straight and pointed. "There it is! Just like it said in Ududu's letters." He'd made Anna read missives from his grandfather over and over and absorbed every detail.

Anna's heart raced as she spotted the sign for Walker Mill that looked just like the one at home, marking the turnoff to the property. "You're right, Josh." She squeezed his shoulder, and he turned a brilliant smile up to her. He kicked his legs under the wagon seat, as if doing so would make them go faster.

Indeed, with a grin, Gage flicked the reins and clicked to the team, and their pace increased. Josh wasn't the only one bursting with anticipation. It was all Anna could do to keep her aching rump on the wagon bench. Nausea and weeks of travel were forgotten in the anticipation of seeing her loved ones. They wouldn't be expecting them. Though they had written and even sent an update from along the journey, many letters got lost. And they might even arrive ahead of any correspondence. What if her family wasn't at home?

But as they rumbled up to a cluster of log cabins surrounding a mill perched on a rocky bank above a chattering creek, a young girl working in a verdant garden—surely, one of Anna's nieces, though it was hard to tell under the floppy sunbonnet—spotted them and ran to the largest home. Dogs barked, chickens flapped, and within moments, two stalwart and heart-squeezingly familiar figures appeared on the porch.

"Edoda." The name left Anna's lips on a breath. Her fingers tightened on her son's shoulder. "Josh, that is your *ududu*. And your uncle Crow." She lifted her hand to wave, though her father and half brother stood unmoving as though still absorbing her arrival.

"*Edutsi.*" Josh corrected her with the solemnity of a schoolteacher.

"Yes. Edutsi. Uncle. And you're right...now would be a good time to practice your Cherokee." She wanted her family to know she had not forgotten.

Gage pulled up on the reins and set the brake. "Son, let me help your mother down first."

The warning proved unnecessary, as Agidoda clapped his hands together and thundered down the porch steps. Within moments, his strong arms lifted her to the ground. He drew her into an embrace that brought tears to her eyes as the familiar scent of his special blend of tobacco wafted around her.

"Uwetsiageyv." Daughter. She'd wondered if she'd ever hear

the word again. His strong fingers tightened on her back against her shoulder blades. "You are really here."

She drew back long enough to wipe the tears from her eyes and observe those that rolled unchecked down her father's face. "Did you not get my letter? The one we sent from Memphis?"

He shook his head. The bright sunlight caught more silver threads among the black than she remembered. "Only the one you wrote before you departed. We figured it would be the end of this month, not the first."

"Travel conditions are improved." Not wishing to begin their visit by lamenting the past, Anna turned to her half brother, who now stood behind Agidoda. "Crow. You look well."

"You also. Motherhood becomes you." He embraced her as their father stepped back to wipe his face, but openly, without shame.

"Thank you, though it did not feel that way early this morning." Anna flushed and pressed her hand over her abdomen.

Her father's eyebrows shot up. "Oh! The Lord be praised. Another grandchild. But I have not met the first." He turned to face Josh, who Gage set down from the wagon. "This must be my namesake."

The three-year-old approached his grandfather with all the dignity of a grown man. "Joshua Garrison Edmonds, sir." He held out his hand, and Anna's father shook it with a hearty laugh. Anna could not remember the last time she had seen him display such emotion. But she was overcome with joy herself...and with tears that would not cease springing from her eyes.

Family surrounded them, and there were hugs all around. Crow dispatched his daughter to run up the lane and spread the news of their arrival. Ned came out of the mill, though Anna didn't recognize him at first. She stared at him with her hands clasped beneath her chin. "Can it be? Ned? You must have grown a foot."

"It's me, Aunt Anna." His deep voice gave her another start.

"Goodness. You're a man." She reached up to hug him. "And running the mill on your own."

"Uncle Joshua still helps in season. It is thanks to him and you that I know all I do."

"Will you show me?" Anna brightened at the prospect of touring the business her family had secured a loan to build a year prior.

"Nothing would give me more pleasure."

"And Josh? He will want to come too. He is our best helper back home." She bent and extended her hand to her son.

"Of course." Ned flashed a bright white smile at his cousin. "We tried to build the new Walker Mill as much like the first one as possible. You can tell me what is the same and what is different." With a gesture, he bid them follow him to the tall frame structure.

All dignity forgotten, Josh broke free of Anna's grasp and went skittering sideways like a creek crab beside his so-grown-up-but-young-enough-to-be-fascinating cousin, talking faster than a snake-oil salesman. Anna laughed and followed at a slower pace, accommodating her loosening and wagon-jostled joints. She left Gage to converse with the men as they tended the horses.

Anna followed the boys around the mill long enough to appreciate that it was just as sturdy and efficient as the one she had inherited. She declined joining their inspection of the grain elevator and fan system in the stuffy attic. She was standing by the window that overlooked the water from the raceway turning the wooden wheel, inhaling the scents of fresh pine and cornmeal that put her in mind of home, when a halloo from below brought her to attention.

Could it be? Last she had heard from Peggy, the Campbells

had settled in Park Hill, where her old friend let out two rooms, boarding house style, in their sizeable log home. Plenty of important people visited the town where Chief Ross made his home. It was near enough, but there was no way Peggy could have gotten here this fast.

Still, Anna hurried to the steps and peered down onto the main floor. And there stood her dearest friend, as fashionable in her pale-green summer lawn dress as if she'd just come from a picnic. "Peggy!" She nearly tripped in her haste to descend into her friend's arms.

"Now, don't you go falling." Mirth and affection thickened Peggy's admonition. "From what I heard, there's more than just you to worry about now."

"It's true." Anna drew back to beam at her. "I'm due in November."

"And you'll be here for the birth!" Peggy squealed and squeezed her shoulders. "I'm going to spoil you rotten."

"No. We're going to be busy. So busy." Anna grasped her hand. "You must come see what I brought."

"Oh. Very well." After retrieving a basket she had left by the door, Peggy allowed herself to be pulled along. They crossed the clearing to where the men unloaded the wagon.

"How did you get here so quickly?"

"Miranda came to fetch me." Peggy gestured to Crow's daughter, who had returned to the garden, filling a split-oak basket with snap beans under the watchful gaze of a home-spun-clad scarecrow. "She knew I was delivering some food just up the way to her aunt's mother, who has been ill. I have too much time on my hands. I enjoy helping out where I can in the community now that I have no inn to tend."

"That will change soon." Anna drew her over to the wagon. Gage and her relatives had cleared enough of their luggage and supplies to uncover the loose board that she could raise to reveal the hidden compartment he'd built in behind the seat. "I saw a lot for sale in Tahlequah that would be perfect for a hotel. Close to the capital square but adjacent to quiet homes. Enough room for a stable."

"Do you mean...? Did you bring...?" Both of Peggy's questions trailed off and ended in a gasp as Anna lifted the board to reveal three clay pots. Peggy covered her mouth. "Anna! You dared to bring all that with you? But the danger you exposed yourself to..."

"Of course, we did. We would not dream of coming without it. Now you can build your inn, and Agidoda can repay the loan he took for this property." Anna stood back and smiled as Gage and her father descended the cabin steps to join them.

Gage came over and rubbed her back. "We only wish we could have brought the belongings of every member of the tribe. But in the interest of concealing the treasure and the weight of the load, we limited ourselves to yours, Mrs. Campbell, the Walkers', and the chief's."

"It will remove a burden from my shoulders." Agidoda extended his hand to Gage, and they shook on it. "Thank you, my son. You have fulfilled your destiny and given our people a new start."

"Not yet." Gage stepped back with his brows knit together. "The Thompsons were expelled from the county after serving their jail time, as promised. And your distant relatives who purchased your inn are keeping it up well, Mrs. Campbell. Yet we've had more than one settler nosing around the mill property after dark, having heard of the buried gold. We will remain vigilant until all of it can be reclaimed."

"That may be many years yet." Anna's father frowned. "Most of our people lack the funds to make the journey, and you know how long it takes. It means everything to us that you have taken a year out of your lives in Georgia to come visit and bring what is ours."

"We haven't taken a year out," Anna insisted. "We've added

one. With you. And I wouldn't have it any other way." She wrapped an arm around her best friend and her father.

Joy filled her at the thought of sharing the growth of her own family with her Cherokee family. One day, with the rise of steam engines, maybe traveling across the country would be easier, and they could visit more often. Until then, she and Gage and their children would guard what was left behind until all their people could flourish with a new beginning.

~

Turn the page for a sneak peek of The Schoolmarm and the Miner, the next book in the Twenty-Niners of the Georgia Gold Rush series!

SNEAK PEEK: THE SCHOOLMARM AND THE MINER

*JUNE **1839***
ATHENS, GEORGIA

Adelaide Duncan approached her headmistress's office with a thrill of anticipation. She'd met with Mrs. Calhoun countless times over the two years she'd attended Cobbham Institute for Young Ladies—to consult on classes, propose student organizations, or to chart her future. After all, the institute was much more than a finishing school, offering classes that ranged from languages to astronomy and philosophy. Always, Addie had been a model student, applying herself with dedication and vigor equal to any male student across town at Franklin College. Always, she'd stayed the course. And now the goal was in sight—freedom. She'd grasp it on the other side of that door.

Addie paused and drew a breath to steady her racing pulse. Mrs. Calhoun prized punctuality and neatness, so Addie had given herself plenty of time to tame her springy brown curls into a low chignon before donning her smartest outfit. She tucked a rebellious lock back under her white bonnet and smoothed the folds of her blue cotton gown that flared from her matching wide belt with its filigree buckle.

She also smoothed her expression. She mustn't look too eager. She'd passed her teacher's examination at the top of her class, and her subsequent interview with Cobbham's board had ended with all but an assurance that she would be selected to fill the opening for the language and literature instructor for the next school year.

Mrs. Calhoun's assistant took her hesitation for nerves and spoke from the desk behind her. "It's all right, Miss Duncan. Mrs. Calhoun is expecting you."

Addie shot a grateful smile over her shoulder at the young woman. "Thank you. Just taking a moment to compose myself."

The girl bobbed her head of slicked-back dark hair. "It's a big day, miss." Her eyes sparkled from behind her spectacles.

Addie's stomach fluttered. Even the secretary thought Addie a shoo-in. She knocked lightly, turned the knob, and entered.

At Addie's appearance, Mrs. Calhoun looked up from some papers spread across her walnut desk. Her black silk dress rustled as she rose. Though husbandless for going on fifteen years, the headmistress remained in widow's weeds—probably because the somber garb enhanced her position of authority. "Good afternoon, Miss Duncan. Pray, have a seat."

Addie blinked. *Miss Duncan*? Since her graduation, Mrs. Calhoun had used Addie's Christian name. Well, she had called her *Adelaide*. When Addie hesitated, the middle-aged educator gestured to a chair facing her desk. Her kind smile unglued Addie's feet.

"Thank you for seeing me." She took a seat, folding her hands over her reticule in her lap. "I will confess, I've been on pins and needles since my interview. I...trust the board was satisfied by my responses?"

The questions the panel of four posed had certainly been thorough, delving not only into how she would handle a classroom but vetting her personal life. Addie had answered them all with her head held high. She'd organized charity outreaches through the school, was an active member of the Presbyterian church, and even kept Micah Garrison at arm's length. His impending graduation from Franklin College had him envisioning a future together far sooner than she could if she wanted to teach. Which she did. She had no intention of tying herself to a man the minute she grasped a diploma. Not even a mild-mannered chemist.

Mrs. Calhoun resumed her own seat, a massive carved chair framed by a bay window that looked out on the institute's walled garden. The gentle sway of powder-pink mimosa blossoms just outside the middle window put Addie at ease. As a member of the faculty, she would have the option of deducting a negligible portion of her monthly pay to lodge here. The third-story room might be small, sparse, and hot until autumn settled over the piedmont region, but it would offer one thing her spacious and well-appointed room at home did not—security. Plus, maybe a view of the garden.

Was it just Addie's eagerness, or was the headmistress taking an inordinately long time to reply? And she was shuffling her papers. "Ahem. Yes. The board found you an exemplary candidate, as you have been an exemplary student. You were their first choice for the position by a long shot."

Addie took a deep breath and could not suppress the smile that broke over her face. "It's pleased I am to hear that, ma'am." Occasionally, her father's brogue snuck across her tongue—most often when emotions ran high, one way or the other.

"That was...until..." Mrs. Calhoun's expression clouded. She fingered a document and peered at Addie as one might a turtle on its back. "Until a report affecting you surfaced. Just yesterday, in fact."

"A...report?" Addie's thoughts raced back through her interactions at Cobbham. The teachers had praised her diligence, the students her generous nature. Was there someone who had secretly held her good name against her? Perhaps Matilda Johnson, who had stood second to Addie on exam day. The girl had offered her congratulations as quickly as she had her praise all year—but behind it lurked the veiled resentment of one who uses another to get ahead. "What kind of report?"

"One regarding your father, I'm afraid."

Addie's heart sank to her toes. "What about him?" That the question came out in a whisper betrayed her fears.

Did you enjoy this book? We hope so!
Would you take a quick minute to leave a review where you purchased the book?
It doesn't have to be long. Just a sentence or two telling what you liked about the story!

~

Love Christian Historical Romance?
Looking for your next favorite book?
Become a Wild Heart Books insider and receive a FREE ebook and get exclusive updates on new releases before anyone else.
Sign up for our newsletter now.
https://wildheartbooks.org/newsletter

AUTHOR'S NOTE

The second book in The Twenty-Niners of the Georgia Gold Rush series had less to do with sluice boxes, boom towns, and hidden mining tunnels and more to do with the native people displaced by that rabid search for riches. While penning a story that includes the Cherokee Removal was not an easy task, to ignore it would have been a grave disservice.

While living near Cumming and Canton, I learned the history of Fort Buffington and the legends of lost Cherokee gold. Yes, many of these are just that...legends. But there were enough of them to raise this researcher's appetite for historical gold—facts long buried by time. Where was Fort Buffington located? What about the Red Bank village? And what happened during the months leading up to the Trail of Tears?

In my quest for knowledge, I consulted endless online resources, visited Canton's Cherokee County History Museum (special thanks to Stephanie Joyner for showing me the private research collection), and read many books. These sources ranged from the broad (*The Georgia Gold Rush* by David Williams) to the specific (*Carrying off the Cherokee: History of Buffington's Company Georgia Mounted Militia* by John W. Latty,

Trail of Tears Round-up Routes by Larry Vogt, and Rev. Charles Walker's extensive Footprints Series) to the legend-based (*Cry of the Eagle: History and Legends of the Cherokee Indians and Their Buried Treasures* by Forest C. Wade). Some questions I was able to answer definitively. Others, not so much. Still others, I fictionalized for the story.

After consulting many sources, including expert researchers in Cherokee County, I placed Fort Buffington fronting the Alabama Road on the north side. I could best visualize this by pinpointing lots 989-946 on the 1895 Bullock map. In choosing a location for Walker Mill, I created a fictional tributary of Mill Creek (as named on an 1867 map, though the same creek appeared to be called Town Creek by 1895 and included a Wilson Mill almost due south of Buffington).

For scenes in the mill, I drew on my brief stint as a historical interpreter for Gwinnett County, including working at pre-Civil War Freeman's Mill. Gristmills were such an integral part of 1800s communities, yet seem underrepresented in fiction, so it was satisfying to write a story set at one.

The legend of the Red Bank gold was a bit harder to unravel. According to oral tales disseminated in the area and *Cry of the Eagle*, whose author claimed to have spent time in the early part of the 1900s with his part-Cherokee grandfather, Chief Rising Fawn had jurisdiction over this area of Georgia, including a dozen or more lower chiefs. After the Treaty of New Echota, he was purported to have called a meeting and invited Cherokee blood brother Jacob Scudder to be caretaker of the wealth of the Hightower Indians (as depicted in the story). A tunnel of two hundred feet was constructed to hide the gold, and each tribe created a network of sign trails over some 250,000 acres. The tunnel featured slab doors to hide the vaults and an overhead deadfall designed to release a large stone by a stone trigger. Work was done in 1836 and 1837, with the treasure not deposited until the Cherokee were certain they had to leave.

Only the Red Bank chief protested Rising Fawn's plan, not trusting Scudder. Wade places the tribe of about a hundred members a mile north of the Hightower/Etowah River along Red Bank Creek (later known as Bannister Creek). They were said to have buried their gold dust in clay pots weighing from six to over forty pounds in twenty-five locations along Bannister and Bruton/Brewton creeks. They also used a cave with a narrow tunnel of about twenty feet into the side of a hill. A deposit weighing thirty-seven pounds was found in 1932 by Roy Tippins. Another account mentions three boys playing near Bannister Creek who found a huge granite rock with strange markings. They were denied permission to dig by the farmer who owned the land, F.R. Grover. They returned at night and dug up a clay pot with nuggets and jewelry worth over fifteen thousand dollars at the time. Grover found out and sued them for the prize...and won.

Years later, a Cumming man who spent weeks with his grandfather while growing up told of a caravan of wagons that arrived in 1909. The Cherokees in these wagons camped at Heardsville for three weeks, then moved two miles northwest of Frogtown before leaving as unexpectedly as they had come. They were said to be descendants of the Red Bank Cherokees who recovered almost $250,000 in gold.

The testimony of a Red Bank resident, John Wright, recorded by General Coffee in 1829 appears to disprove the aforementioned location of the village. Wright testified that his town lay on both sides of the Hightower/Etowah River six miles above Sixes settlement and mine (thus, considerably west of the Wade location). Hickory Log Village was two miles northeast of Red Bank Village, and the town of Canton was established between them on the south side of the river. Multiple maps, including many in the trusted Footprints Series, confirm this location. Therefore, with the preponderance of authentic information, I went with this location for my story and had the Red Bank leaders choose Walker Creek as the place to hide their gold due to the connection to Anna's father. I leave it with you, my reader, to further research and satisfy your own curiosity in this matter.

Real characters with cameo appearances included Captain Ezekiel Buffington, Lieutenant Warren Clayton, Assistant Quartermaster Private John Wood, and Private Newton Perkins, whose stepfather, Moses, owned the land on which Fort Buffington was built. Reverend Evan Jones and Brother Jesse Bushyhead were also ministers serving the Baptist circuit through Cherokee County during the 1830s. Finally, the love story of Sarah Ridge and Lieutenant George Paschal, which served as an inspiration for Gage's courtship of Anna, was true.

Some events in the book were inspired by real history as well, including the stickball game, the terms of interpreters hired by the militia, and Gage's measles scare. In May of 1838, Private Pickens Reynolds went to see the new doctor at the fort for this complaint. At the grocery two hundred yards away, he drank sweet brandy to bring the measles out, then he was medicated, bled, given rice gruel, and had cream of tartar put on his eyes for two weeks.

Harassment of the Cherokees by white settlers was also based on real incidents. In December of 1837, a man named Bell stole the fish trap of James Proctor and attempted to take his gun, but failing, struck him on the head with a stone and knocked him out. The next day, Bell went to the home of Proctor's son and took a gun. Finally, the lottery claimant of Widow Ragsdale's house destroyed her corn by turning his hogs into the field at night, then sowed wheat in its place. Reverend Evans worked to right these wrongs.

I'd like to thank the team at Wild Heart Books—including my publisher, Misty M. Beller; my editor, Janyre Tromp; Sarah

Erredge and Sherri Wilson Johnson—for their skill and vision in helping me bring this story to my readers. Also my launch team, especially my beta readers. And you, my amazing readers, who love history as much as I do and support me as an author so well. Remember, you can find Denise Weimer books under Denise Farnsworth, my new married name, now!

If you enjoyed The Maiden and the Mountie, your reviews let publishers know my stories are worth continuing to publish. I notice and treasure each one. I'd also love to connect with you online.

Newsletter signup: https://webs.us19.list-manage.com/subscribe?u=16c561f75e5036405879c9836&id=b58acc62a5

Website: https://denisefarnsworthbooks.mailchimpsites.com/

Facebook: https://www.facebook.com/denise.farnsworth.books

Twitter: https://x.com/denise_farnsw

Coming in November 2026, the final installment of The Twenty-Niners of the Georgia Gold Rush:

The Schoolmarm and the Miner

1839

A grieving sheriff in hiding. A schoolteacher on a mission. In Georgia's untamed gold country, second chances shimmer where hearts are most broken.

Sheriff **Wade Coulter** hung up his gun belt the day he failed to capture the man responsible for killing his sister. Now a broken widower raising his daughter in the North Georgia mountains, he buries his guilt beneath the weight of a gold miner's pick and the comfort of a bottle. He's got no time for do-gooders...especially not the prim new schoolteacher bent on reforming his little girl and his drinking habits.

Adelaide Duncan arrives in the upstart gold-mining town of Dahlonega with the righteous zeal of reform. Not only will she educate the children—she'll join a temperance society that will save miners and ne'er-do-wells from the stranglehold of alcohol that destroyed her father. She'll also marry the assistant assayer at the new U.S. mint—if she can prevent herself from falling asleep at the altar. And if she can quit thinking about the haunted and handsome Wade Coulter and his adorable-if-spirited daughter.

Then a deadly cave-in and the discovery of corruption at a local assaying office force Wade and Addie into a dangerous alliance. When threats to Addie's life surface and Wade's old enemy returns, he must decide whether to pick up his badge—or lose the woman who's brought his heart back to life.

ABOUT THE AUTHOR

North Georgia native Denise Weimer, now Denise Farnsworth, has authored around twenty traditionally published novels and novellas--historical and contemporary romance, romantic suspense, and time slip. As a freelance editor and Acquisitions & Editorial Liaison for Wild Heart Books, she's helped other authors reach their publishing dreams. A wife and mother of two wonderful daughters, Denise always pauses for coffee, chocolate, and old houses.

You can visit Denise at https://denisefarnsworthbooks. mailchimpsites.com/, and connect with her on social media.

Monthly e-mail list: https://webs.us19.list-manage.com/subscribe?u=16c561f75e5036405879c9836&id=b58acc62a5

If you love historical romance, check out the other Wild Heart books!

A Winter at the White Queen by Denise Weimer

In the world of the wealthy, things are never quite as they appear.

Ellie Hastings is tired of playing social gatekeeper—and poor-relation companion—to her Gibson Girl of a cousin. But her aunt insists Ellie lift her nose out of her detective novel long enough to help gauge the eligibility of bachelors during the winter social season at Florida's Hotel Belleview. She finds plenty that's mysterious about the suave, aloof Philadelphia inventor, Lewis Thornton. Why does he keep sneaking around the hotel? Does he have a secret sweetheart? And what is his connection to the evasive Mr. Gaspachi, slated to perform at Washington's Birthday Ball?

Ellie's comical sleuthing ought to put Lewis out, but the diffident way her family treats her smashes a hole in his normal reserve. When Florence Hastings's diamond necklace goes missing, Ellie's keen mind threatens to uncover not only Lewis's secrets, but give him back hope for love.

~

A Counterfeit Betrothal by Denise Weimer

A frontier scout, a healing widow, and a desperate fight for peace.

At the farthest Georgia outpost this side of hostile Creek Territory in 1813, Jared Lockridge serves his country as a scout to redeem his father's botched heritage. If he can help secure peace against Indians allied to the British, he can bring his betrothed to the home he's building and open his cabinetry shop. Then he comes across a burning cabin and a traumatized woman just widowed by a fatal shot.

Freed from a cruel marriage, Esther Andrews agrees to winter at the Lockridge homestead to help Jared's pregnant sister-in-law. Lame in one foot, Esther has always known she is second-hand goods, but the gentle carpenter-turned-scout draws her heart with as much skill as he creates furniture from wood. His family's love offers hope even as violence erupts along the frontier—and Jared's investigation into local incidents brings danger to their doorstep. Yet how could Esther ever hope a loyal man like Jared would choose her over a fine lady?

If you love historical romance, check out the other Wild Heart books!

Rescue in the Wilderness by Andrea Byrd

William Cole cannot forget the cruel burden he carries, not with the pock marks that serve as an outward reminder. Riddled with guilt, he assumed the solitary life of a long hunter, traveling into the wilds of Kentucky each year. But his quiet existence is changed in an instant when, sitting in a tavern, he overhears a man offering his daughter—and her virtue—to the winner of the next round of cards. William's integrity and desire for redemption will not allow him to sit idly by while such an injustice occurs.

Lucinda Gillespie has suffered from an inexplicable illness her entire life. Her father, embarrassed by her condition, has subjected her to a lonely existence of abuse and confinement. But faced with the ultimate betrayal on the eve of her eighteenth birthday, Lucinda quickly realizes her trust is better placed in his hands of the mysterious man who appears at her door. Especially when he offers her the one thing she never thought would be within her grasp—freedom.

In the blink of an eye, both lives change as they begin the difficult, danger-fraught journey westward on the Wilderness Trail. But can they overcome their own perceptions of themselves to find love and the life God created them for?